Threat To The World

"Money Talks, But Love Talks Louder"

By: Richard Spraggins

Richard Spraggins

ISBN-13:978-1974399659
ISBN-10:1974399656

Cover Design: Crystell Publications
Book Productions: Crystell Publications
We Help You Self Publish Your Book

ACKNOWLEDGMENTS

First and foremost a special thanks to my mother for the tremendous support. Without you this project would not have been possible. I appreciate the first proof reading (although you be chopping up my work like Edward Scissor Hands, lol.) By the same token I'm overly thankful for everything that you do. At the end of the day we can say we did this project together. Yup-Yup!

I would like to launch my gratitude to the highest degree to Crystell Publications. If you never heard it before I am proud to be the first to tell you Crystal – you're the truth! I know that's not the first time you heard that. For real though, thank you for everything that you do for the inside and outside communities. For the free world you are a gift from God. For us currently on lock, you are a dream maker (not a dream crusher) and I speak for everyone in here who's Pimp'n, T-money, Julian (Fatz) Burt. their pen – You Are Appreciated!

To all my cronies on lock who I build with on a daily basis and anyone who I ever had a meaningful conversation with – Thank You! There's a term in TDCJ that's overrated and used to describe "us" as a whole; Y'all! If the ignorance floats deep in the beast then y'all are responsible.

If the CO's talk to us as if we're one of their kids at home then y'all are responsible. For this reason G-No, F Money, Fatz, Kenny the Barber, 44, Lil D, Giant, Cliff, Skinner, Randy (Ra Ra) Arroyo, Dragoo, Black, Duce, South Bank Don Busta Bust (AKA) Jonathan Nickerson. My facilitator – Scrappy (AKA) Matthew Salazar. Drow and my cousin Sylvester Spraggins (AKA Chaos) the whole horizon is "y'all". Make sure your influence radiates a mirror effect to the unlighted because "we" can change the dynamics of how they view the criminal sitting next to you. Do something great!

I Dedicate This Novel To The Love Of My Life: Shanna Marie Hubbard

Preface

Thomas Threat "who prefers to be called by his last name," is the offspring of a well-known Midwest pimp. Threat is on lock down in the Texas Department of Criminal Justice system (TDCJ) on a twelve year bid. While there, he runs into Mack who laces him up with the essential requirements needed in order to succeed, not only in the inside but on the outside as well.

Threat's beautiful, dynamic and very loyal sister Maya has been by his side from day one. Maya is Threat's biggest fan, but while he is willing to do anything to rekindle what is in his blood, he also has to come to an awakening of what is the most important factor in his life.

In this psychological twist, a saga of reality versus fantasy, Threat will come to understand that the voices inside his head come with the game. Money talks, but love talks louder...Bottom line!

CHAPTER 1
CHOICES

Like most people, I had a Hollywood perception of prison: "Smoked up dorms with tatted and flexed up bodybuilders roaming around with built up hate and shanks." I arrived at the Texas Department of Criminal Justice on a hot Thursday afternoon, and just to keep it hella real, I was shaking like a leafless tree in the middle of fall. I came in weighing a measly buck 35 with a heavy load, sweaty palms and trembling lips. I figured that I just stepped into my worst nightmare. It was like being on stage, amateur night at Showtime at The Apollo. All conversations and dominos came to a halt when I rolled up. Heads bounced in my direction to size me up. Yeah, all eyes on me. My first thought was, keep my ass to the wall and go out swinging. My first impression was twisted because it didn't go down like Shawshank Redemption or anything comparable to American Me.

I was greeted at the cell door by an old school named Mack. He was probably in his mid-fifties and despite prison; he carried the presence of a player who did not have a single worry in the world. He was short and stocky with a big head like a pit bull with a broad face. Mack was blacker than the color black with one single gold tooth to his upper right canine.

I was assigned to the bunk directly across from him, so you know, after a couple of days peeping my isolation and not knowing what to expect, Mack approached me with a cold soda and a photo album. "You look like you need to be laced up." Mack's first words as he tossed me the soda and photo album. Now one thing I learnt from watching movies was not to accept shit from no nigga. Next, he'll be thinking that you owe him something like maybe a favor or two or three. I twisted my face with skepticism which must have been clear because Mack tilted his head back and cracked up laughing.

"Young blood, I ain't on that side of the track. I ain't gonna hurt you and I sho don't want or need anything from you, I come in peace." It was a relief, not basically at what he said, but that soda rolled down my throat in maybe two or three swallows in that hot ass dorm. With my head tilted back, washing away the last drops of soda from the can, I could hear Mack laughing again. "Seems that's just what you needed, a coke and a smile. Now relax your nerves son because I'ma gonna give it to you raw and uncut. It's like this Mack said. "You can live in prison one or two ways. You can serve time or it can serve you."

I stood up from my bunk much taller than Mack but I felt a dominate demeanor from him that was to be respected. I almost called him sir but I kept it simple and asked him. "What you mean big homie?"

3

"You don't have to be Einstein to see that you have a lot to learn. Your green horn ass can easily get caught up in the ignorance that floats inside these walls." He pointed his hand towards the dayroom and broke down the scene.

"You see them clowns in front of that TV, staring at it with their mouths open and looking like zombies in a trance?" I chuckled, "yeah." "Well them same clowns gonna be there until they are told to go to sleep. Goes the same for them talking shit at the domino table, and those over there sitting on their bunks staring at the walls in anger with a big chip on their shoulder because they blaming everybody and they momma for the life they chased. Now, son you got yourself a choice, you can tighten up and make this shit count for something or you can fold and be just like them in that dayroom. I hope you choose resilience and show the world your ability to bounce back."

Mack's word of wisdom was felt no doubt and I could clearly hear and understand each word. My eyes widened larger and larger the more pages I flipped through of his photo album. This nigga had a Rolls Royce Phantom Coupe, a drop top Benz 600 series, a fleet of minks, diamonds, gators and three piece suits, you name it he had it. But here's the hook; all the pictures he's surrounded by nothing but top flight hoes. All the trappings of "American Style and Prosperity." He continued, "You have an opportunity forced upon you to tighten up, get a handle on your flaws, get a free education, and master a talent and trade. It's all up to you young blood because like I said; you got a choice. Believe me, these crackers would love to write you off as crazy and put you on they psych load." I stared at his photo album dumbfounded. Who was this nigga?

From his pictures, I could tell he's somebody. More questions bounced around in my dome. For instance, if he's so gamed and papered up then why was he here? Does he go around preaching this shit to everybody and last but not least, I had to ask him, "What made you approach me?" Mack rubbed his hands together while looking deep into the depths of my soul. With his tight beady eyes he stared hard at me and said, "What I'm trying to lace you up with son is that in order to win and keep your mind sane, you gotta make a conscious choice not to waste your time while you here. Have something to show for when the time comes. Like the old saying: Today is the first day of the rest of your life." Mack took my hand in a handshaking position as if we just agreed on something. Then he finally said, "Pimp recognizes Pimp."

Mack left the Middleton Unit the very next day. Middleton is a transfer facility so he was more likely transferred to an I.D unit with the general population. When I think of old Mack, I'm reminded of seventh grade literature class and a book we had to read titled Brief Encounters. It stressed that sometimes we meet people who we might know only for a hot second but who had a long lasting impact on our lives. Mack was that kind of nigga.

That was twelve years ago. Since then I earned a college degree with more than three hundred credit hours. Yeah, and your man is pursuing a master's degree in psychology on an academic scholarship. I wrote three books, a play, a gang of short stories and poems; all published. I gained an appreciation for art so much so that now my artwork is displayed in stores and online. I invested twenty-five dollars and found myself in the prison craft shop. I'm not one to just roll with the punches so I had to do something a little different. My time in the shop wasn't spent making costume jewelry, leather boots, saddles, and belts for C.O's on a bullshit commission; I went in a totally different direction. I took my art skills to the next level and got into commercial art; helping companies in the free world sell their products. I designed a number of illustrations for books, magazines, newspapers and posters. I have a few designs for postage stamps but they haven't been released yet because I'm like Cuba Gooding Jr. when it comes to my skills...SHOW ME THE MONEY!!!

Speaking of money, after TDCJ got their cut, me helping my sister with bills and what not, I was still able to save sixty stacks over the course of twelve years. One thing Mack said that stuck in my head was, "have something to show for when the time comes." I noticed how niggas in here couldn't wait to spend their money. When they called commissary some of these niggas looked like bitches running to the nearest clearance sale. Even their expressions had "Fiend" written all over it and for what? Junk food? Hell nah, I saved my duckets by limiting my habits to none. I don't drink coffee and I don't have a sweet tooth, nor do I have the desire to make spreads (prison buffet made with whatever the inmates has stored in their cell, most often a Ramen noodles mix.) I went to the window maybe once every other month and that was for basic essentials like hygiene and writing materials.

So what did I do in my spare time? Truth be told, there's no such thing as spare time when you're on a mission, every minute, every second counts. I didn't have the luxury to watch TV, talk shit and play games. So, I read every book under the sun and studied everything from the Roman Empire to Ancient Egypt. Studied every known religion, from Islam to Scientology. Read about everyone from Marcus Garvey to Karl Marx. Even Pimp Ken and Bishop Don Juan because when it comes to knowledge you have to be open minded to everything in order to understand the universal spiritual laws of nature. I now speak fluent Spanish because knowing another language is the product of understanding a culture arising from cooperative efforts required by societies. In the near future, you will have to know Spanish in order to work at McDonald's.

Some people say it's conceited to brag about your physical appearance. The way I see it is, whoever said that shit must look like who done it, what for and please don't do it no more. Here I am 34 years old and in the best shape of my life, yes sir, and it's all because I made fitness and nutrition a priority in my life even in this hellhole. My physique is on point because I was determined not to be that 135 lb. soaking wet weakling I was twelve years ago. Now at six, one I'm chiseled and ripped, added muscle to this 195 lbs. immaculate body frame. I take my body serious because it's my temple and the foundation of everything I'm about.

I'm feeling live because tomorrow is my release.

I rode on the Blue Bird with a crazy tatted up Mexican

who talked about prison with the same enthusiasm that most niggas would save for either sports or pussy. I wasn't going to sit up here and share war stories with this fool so while he was running his mouth and the Blue Bird was flying like a bat outta hell, I stared at a postcard I received from Mack around seven years ago. It simply said: Don't waste time learning the tricks of the trade, instead learn 'The Trade', and don't fold cause them crackers can't wait to put you on they psych load (that way they can keep making money off you).

The message was symbolic no doubt. I most definitely mastered 'The Trade' and I certainly am not on anybody's psych load. But, I can't even lie because I do have a small case of hallucination issues going on. I hear voices from time to time and it's a trip because sometimes I consider Mack like a supernatural messenger sent by the Game God, so maybe it's his voice I hear calling my name. The postage was sent from Dallas, Texas where I fell from so maybe one day we'll bump heads again but today I'm headed to an entirely different city.

My sister copped a house in Orange, Texas and from what I know, that's somewhere in between Beaumont and Louisiana. We are originally from Minneapolis, Minnesota and if you don't know, that's the Gopher State, which is northeast central of the Midwest, residing next to Lake Superior and a hop and skip away from Canada. 'The Igloo' is the proper name for Minneapolis in the hood and I suppose that's self-explanatory because it's colder than a muthafucka there.

Twelve years ago, I had the misfortune of messing with

Texas and found myself locked up in a Dallas jail cell. A couple of my Igloo niggas was pushing work with a direct link from the south to the north and I was caught slipping by myself. All I remember seeing were AR15 rifles and Sig P226 sidearm when DEA came blasting through the door. Being from Minnesota and I wouldn't talk and the judge felt like I was a flight risk so bail was denied. Yeah, even despite my clean record.

My sister Maya moved to Texas to be closer to me, so it's no secret that we have a tight bond that in no way could ever be compromised. She is two years younger than I am but sometimes on the real; she acts like she's my mom's. So much so that she even suggested I discharge to Orange, insisting that it's the perfect place and opportunity to get on my feet. She even talks like a parole officer because she claims that a big city like Minneapolis or Dallas can trigger old habits and place me at risk for reoffending. Feel me? But, it's all good; baby sis is over protective because she's grabbed grips with reality that when it comes to family we are all we have left.

My old man was a well-respected pimp from Chi, and my mom's? Well she was his bottom bitch. After my old man found out through a DNA test that me and Maya are actually his shorties and not some trick babies, they relocated to Minneapolis to square up. Maya was six and I was eight when they were both mysteriously burned to death in a small house on the south side while we were at school. Up until we were 18, we were raised by the Hennepin Youth Center.

I carry my old man's name, Thomas Threat. Only

difference, he went by Double T but I simply go by my last name, Threat!

My mom's on the other hand is a full blooded white girl who's birth name was Samantha Richardson, but very well known as Star on the street. It don't take a rocket scientist to figure out that me and Maya are mix breeds. Which in Minneapolis is no big deal it is as common as a common cold, but here in Texas we manage to raise a few eyebrows to more than a few racist hick muthafucker's when they fully grasp the understanding that there's a few more Barack Obama's floating around.

CHAPTER 2
THREAT TO SOCIETY

A couple hours later after I departed the speeding Blue Bird with the tatted up Mexican we spent the night at the Walls Unit. I hardly slept, I mean I tossed and turned the whole night. Maybe because my anticipation and eagerness to face the world was in fifth gear.

You can only imagine how a horse might feel prior to that door swinging open at the races. The Sport of King's is amongst the most popular spectator sport in the world. Why, because millions are being made with on and off track betting. Do you actually think that the horse knows people are placing bets, going for broke for his triumph? I hardly doubt it. The only thing on his mind is getting around that track. It's most definitely mutual with me ya dig. In fact, whoever is placing bets it would be in their best interest to roll with me or else face great disappointment.

Today is D Day the day of my release only it's a day earlier than my actual release date. See, today is Thursday but the date online says that I'm scheduled to be released on Friday. But Saturday is the 4th of July and in TDCJ they

11

start the 4th of July weekend on Friday, so everybody that was scheduled to get out on Friday leaves today. You with me? A'ight, because if you understand then you would know that gives me the opportunity to surprise my sister. Yeah, her computer literate ass is somewhere online counting down the days, but only this time I got the ups on her.

After my property was inventoried and placed in a red chain bag. I was dressed out in a blue auto mechanics shirt with the name 'Pablo' on the name tag. Also I was given a pair of brown slacks and a pair of Jackie Chan karate shoes. Only these karate shoes had an extra-large sole, adding a couple inches to my height. I was greeted at a window by a fresh off the boat looking nigga. Must be African from his accent and reeking odor coming from the window. I can't believe TDCJ allows them niggas to work under them foul ass conditions: must be some type of safety hazard or something. Damn!

Before I bounced with my fifty-dollar check, bus ticket and signing a few papers, the African guard said with an attitude that a check for sixty thousand dollars would be mailed to my sister's address no later than two weeks. He had to double check and went out of his way to confirm it with his supervisor before telling me though. As if a young, black, talented and educated nigga who's actually from America can't be rolling with them type of numbers on their account. Since my bid I experienced them Africans to be some of the most judgmental, stereotypical muthafucker's alive. They won't even go to the nearest CVS and purchase any damn deodorant.

Hey, but I wasn't plexing though because the sight of the freshly polished 'Golden Gates' immediately took that funky ass nigga off my mental. The gates lead to a two-way glass door which was the only thing separating me from freedom. I never imagined that a mere glass door could look so good. It looked like the stairway to heaven or even a portal to another dimension. I increased my speed, in my zone, in my own lane, I left everyone else behind. This is my time to shine. I know because I'm equipped with dangerous weapons that have to be reckon with. A brain, physical greatness, focus and a vision. I manipulated the system now it's time to up my strategy and finesse the world. Therefore, I will live up to my name because I know that I am not a menace but only a 'Threat to Society'.

CHAPTER 3
"MORE THAN MEETS THE EYE"

I cashed the fifty-dollar check at a liquor store two blocks from the Walls Unit. Right off, I noticed that it was supposed to be a liquor store but also catered to inmates who were being released from prison. Fresh triple x white t's on racks along with muscle shirts, denim jeans, shorts and fresh icy white socks and they also had a package deal. For fifty bucks, you can get a pint of crown, an outfit that includes an Acne t-shirt and dickies, a carton of cigarettes and a crisp white hat with your city on the front. There were several rows of hats with D Town, H Town, San Antonio, West, and East Texas on the front. They even had Black N Mild's and Grape Swisher Sweets on a two for one special with synthetic K2 weed products sold under the counter.

I read in prison that the Middle Easterners got the game from the Asians and the Asians got the game from the Jews. Studying a niggas's spending habits is the best revenue. Damn, and I was witnessing the shit right here in my face. The Middle Easterner asked me in a heavy accent.

"You want white t my nigga with name on front?" I didn't trip, I just politely got my cash and change from the counter top and opened the front door and after the bells above my head stopped ringing, I said, "Capitalism exist free of government restraints."

He looked confused so I threw him the deuces and kept it moving. I used the bus voucher and made my way to Orange, Texas. I didn't like the idea of hopping on another bus considering that crazy ass ride on the Blue Bird. But, I wasn't shell shocked, I was only determined to get to my destination so another bus ride wouldn't be shit. It was even pretty live kicking it with a few badass kids for a change.

A woman who resembled Precious sat on the aisle across to the left by herself because she was too large to share an aisle with anyone else. However, I linked up with her shorties;

"Are you Mexican?"

"Why do you have a fruit sack with your stuff in it?"

"Are you going to work?"

"Are you homeless?"

Yeah, they drilled me with the 50 cent, twenty-one questions but I was not a bit irritated. I understand that shorties are the most inquisitive creatures on this planet so whatever comes to the dome, they gonna ask. I couldn't answer all their questions at once though; besides I had a better idea. I reached in my red bag and found my fifth edition encyclopedia. They must be accustomed to the twenty-first century way of viewing shit because the frowns on their faces when they seen the book stated: Nigga who reads books, this is 2015. If it wasn't a video game or a touch screen gadget then it wasn't cool. But, I was bent on showing them that there's a lot of ways to be informed without depending on the internet. They were all big eyed when I showed them who Helen Keller was.

The older boy said in a low whisper so his mom's couldn't hear, "You gotta be shitting me, she was deaf and blind at the same time?

"Yeah lil man" I said. "And still she overpowered her disabilities by learning how to read and write, graduated from college with honors and wrote a couple of books."

"Wow," The little girl said but I had a lot more to show them.

I showed them people and miracles that they never known to exist. Not even black history! For this reason, I broke them off a brief history lesson and showed them that a slave by the name of Booker T. Washington became a U.S educator, Frederick Douglas escaped only to come back to buy his freedom, Harriet Tubman helped over 300 slaves to freedom, Malcom X wanted to fight, Martin Luther King had a dream, Langston Hughes assumed Harlem Renaissance and Alex Haley made a movie about it all.

Around an hour or so of lacing them up of with who they were and where they came from, they were knocked out sleep. Since they were headed for Houston, my stop came first. Before I bounced I handed their moms a twenty-dollar bill then said, "Ma'am with all due respect, get them a few books because I think they'll cherish it more than the internet."

The lady placed the twenty-dollar bill to her large breast with both hands, then with a big bright smile she said, "I sure will, bless your heart baby." I also gave her the encyclopedia as I exited the bus. It was right before noon when I finally made it to Orange.

I was greeted with a scorching hot temperature, clearly over the 100-degree mark. I couldn't complain though because I rather be hot then cold any day. Minnesota winters will make the average nigga fold up.

The Greyhound bus dropped me off at a Love's Truck stop, overseeing the I-10 freeway, but I pressed east on foot until I reached Denny's. The restaurant was crowded considering it was lunch break hour, so I chilled on a bench outside. I paid attention to people's face's while they were glued to their cell phone screens and it seemed like the entire world had some type of electronic device pulled out. I saw old couples, young couples, and singles with children and employees entering and exiting the restaurant. I guess Denny's must be some type of hot commodity here in this city. Then I see a sign that was intended for the traffic on I-10 to see and I realized why; Buffet $6.99 all you can eat. Off the top, I thought about knocking some grub off but I shook my head as I realized I was good. The only thing on my mind at this point was getting to my sister's crib and if I spent too much money then I might not have enough money to cover a cab fare, so I chilled. Right then as I was reaching in my bag to get my sister's address, I seen a shadow approach me from my peripheral vision. I froze with a sudden stiffening posture but slightly moving my eyes to my back to see who the fuck was behind me.

"So how long did you do?"

Is all I heard as I slowly turned around and witnessed the best eye candy I seen all day. I raised my eyebrows at the sight of a young dime who reminded me of Ariana Grande except she was thicker in all the right places with long curly hair. She was wearing a short red jersey dress with her hair pulled back into a loose ponytail underneath a white visor cap. She was wearing white sandals with her perfect, manicured French tip toenails on display. Everything about her said 'High Maintenance'.

I was eager to get inside her thoughts so I played it off and asked her.

"How long did I do what" (as if I didn't know what she was talking about?)

My clothes and red chain bag was a dead giveaway.

"Uh, don't try to play me, you got on the same silly ass looking shit my brother had on when he got out. Or else you must be the new thrift store king."

I chuckled a little bit as I noticed she most definitely had flavor and attitude, with a country southern drawl. I clenched my hands together and asked her. "Is that a bad thing?" I said half joking.

"I don't know, you tell me. I know you didn't go to prison for being good, now did you?"

"Not at all, not at all." I asked her. "By the way, what's your name?"

"Alisha!"

"That's a beautiful name, it fits you. But dig, Alisha my name is Threat and between you and me prison is only what you make it, and yeah, it could be considered good if you take advantage of it by coming out stronger than you were before you went in. Prison is kinda like an advantage you know; versus the person who is caught up with life and really don't have the time or energy to focus on themselves."

"Ah hell nah." Alisha said with her hand on her hips. "First off, where you from because I know damn well you ain't from around here talking like that? And, what's your real name because you and I both know your momma didn't name you Threat?"

I reached in my back pocket then showed her my TDCJ I.D card as I said, "My name is Threat baby, no gimmicks no tricks. I go by my last name, all great people do. And to answer your question, I'm from Minneapolis but I got caught up in Dallas twelve years ago."

"Twelve years ago?" Alisha asked with bulging eyes. "Oh my God, but you look so young." She was sizing me up, examining my forearms, neck and whatever open skin that was available to her eyes, then she continued, "And you don't have all those stupid tattoos like my brother. He swear up and down he's hard; I won't bore you with the details but what kind of nigga goes around with his shirt off, making it his duty to inform people he's been to prison? I been to prison nigga, I been to prison nigga. OMG, who cares?"

I found myself touching my fingertips together while tapping them in a steeple. I looked at her then said, "I don't know if you noticed or not but um I ain't your brother."

Alisha let out a huge breath of air with her palm pressed

to her heart then said, "Thank God for that." She smacked her lips, then said, "Look I'm gonna be real with you, you being from out of state, you got a head on your shoulders and to top it off, you're one fine specimen, these hoes gonna flock to your ass like flies to shit; she quickly sat down on the bench then scooted closer into my space. She looked up at me with her hazel brown eyes, and while they were focusing on me like a puppy dog, she said, "Just remember who discovered your ass." I cracked up laughing, and then repeated the punch line.

"Discovered my ass?"

"Yeah" she said. No need to front, I discovered you. Besides, these Orange hoes are messy, I mean very messy. Boy you don't even know the half."

Alisha gave me the rundown about Orange and the people that reside there. After all the people and associates, she named, she was telling me to avoid everyone except her. I could tell from her high energy and outspoken personality that she was cool people and that she was just dying to meet someone different.

Sometimes people blow shit out of proportion, but I'm not exaggerating when I tell you that her eyes are hypnotic. Let me paint a picture for you. Have you ever heard the name Sharbat Gula? Nine times out of ten, I missed you, but I'm willing to put sixty stacks on it that you know her face. As a young Afghan girl, she was photographed by a dude name Steve McCurry for the cover of National Geographic in 1985. That image alone went viral and became one of the most iconic shots in the history of photography because of the girl's piercing money green eyes. It's plain as day that Alisha's eyes possess a natural power.

Something like the girl on the National Geographic cover, but with a face and body of a goddess. She's an interesting phenomenon and for some reason I know there's a lot more than meets the eye. She talked for a good twenty minutes while I sat there patiently and listened. She would have kept going, only she snapped to the fact that she was supposed to be doing something entirely different.

"Oh shoot!" She said while standing up quick. "Let me run in here and get my momma's food before she have a fit."

"That's what's up" I said. "I gotta make a call anyway so I'll be in the lobby if you need to holla back." We both made our way into the restaurant, and to be straight up, we were the best-looking couple yet that entered the building. I mean I'm just saying because people were gazing us up and down. I had change from cashing the check in Huntsville so the .75 cent required to make a local call didn't piss me off that much. I dialed my sister's number and patiently waited as I listened to a Beyoncé ring tone.

"I woke up like this, I woke up like this."

It went straight to voice mail. "Hey, you reached Maya Threat and unfortunately I missed your call, but if you would be so sweet to leave a brief message, I will respond at my earliest convenience. If however, you are intending to make a payment, you can go to Mayathreat@chevydealers.com. Thank you, and have a blessed day." Beep.

I see Alisha approaching the lobby with a plastic bag

with what I assume to be her mom's order. So I decided to kill two birds with one stone by leaving a message for my sister and Alisha at the same time.

"What's good sis? To be honest, I was intending to knock on your door and surprise you but things aren't going as planned. This place don't even have a taxi service, transit bus or train. Where in the hell you got me sis?"

I chuckled as I looked into Alisha's eyes; I placed my index finger to my mouth, hinting for her not to say anything, then I continued,

"I'm at Denny's going west from I-10, if you don't pick me up within the next hour or so, then I'm gonna head that way on foot. This place can't be that big. Anyway, love ya, see you in a minute!"

As I slowly placed the phone back to the receiver to hang it up, Alisha said, "Aww that was so sweet. I wish I was close to my brother like that. He gets on my last nerve, I mean like he could have come and got this order for momma. Ain't like he busy, all he doing is playing stupid video games. Anyway, let me press the breaks before I get upset. And what you mean walk? Ain't no nigga that I discovered gonna be walking nowhere. Where your sister live at cause I can drop you off?"

I had the address ready because this part of the play was already predicted. Just as I was about to give it to her, it was like a bulb suddenly turned on inside her dome.

"Threat, Threat, Threat...."

Alisha shot off an exaggerated "Oh", nodding her head as if she just then understood one of the world's great secrets. "I know your sister, Maya Threat. The pretty chick that work at the Chevrolet dealership on MacArthur. Yeah, she sold me my car, she's cool as hell, and I like her. That's right; it all makes sense now because last winter she was saying that people here complain too much, that where she's from we couldn't handle it. I know where she lives at because sometimes I drop my payment off at her house."

She let that sink in for a moment before she pushed on. She said, "Oh, and one more thing."

"What's up?"

"Everybody here knows everybody!"

We laughed and was shooting the shit while we made our way to Alisha's car. It was automatic as if we had natural chemistry with each other. No worries, no stress, just a couple of individuals who just met that in no doubt felt comfortable in each other's presence. While we were walking, I fell back a little and without looking back, she asked me.

"Why you walking so slow?"

I smirked then said, "I'm enjoying the view from back here."

"Yeah, I bet you are" She said as she threw a little bit of an extra switch in her step.

Now I already knew that Alisha was high maintenance just from peeping her French tip toes and fly fingernails. However, when she pushed a button from her key chain to disarm an alarm to a 2015 Cherry Red Camaro Z 28, it threw me for a loop. She was even showing off because she pushed another button and the car started. Then she looked at me with a playful grin and winked her eye as to say; Nigga I bet you haven't ever seen that before. When she opened the door, Rihanna came blasting through the surround sound.

"Don't act like you forgot. Like blah, blah, blah Bitch better have my money"

When I sat in the passenger's seat, I looked around and it reminded me of some shit straight up outta an episode of Nightrider. Black, soft full grain leather, a multimedia center with a custom 14-inch touchscreen, replacing the center console, an electric powered sunroof and a surround sound system, seemed to be coming from everywhere, even the damn seats. She put her mom's order in the back seat on top of a pile of shoeboxes. Prada, Gucci, Jimmy Choo's, Nicholas Kirkwood, Tom Ford. Damn, she most definitely got style and grace that comes with a pretty price tag.

But check game, my legs are long and they were cramped sitting in the passenger's seat so I wanted to scoot the seat back a little. There was only one problem! I couldn't find the adjust button. I asked Alisha over the music, "How do you adjust this seat back?"

She giggled while she was applying lip-gloss to her lips in the rearview mirror, she said, "Dam nigga, what did they have when you was out; Flintstone cars? It's on the console to your left." While I was adjusting the seat back Alisha's phone was lighting up, so she hit the touchscreen to turn Rihanna down. Here's the hook, she also answered the phone from the same touchscreen. Next thing you know, the whole inside interior became a telephone.

"I'm on my way momma."

"What's taking so long? And why you ain't answering your phone, I been trying to call you?"

"Momma, my phone was in the car."

"Well hurry up now girl, Mrs. Woods in dem will be here any minute now to go to choir rehearsal."

"If you woulda had that lazy...

"What was that?"

"Nothing, I'm on my way momma." Was all Alisha said before disconnecting the call.

Soon after, she grabbed her IPhone and texted someone. She looked as if she was up to something because she was cutting her eyes at me from the corner of her eyes. See, at this point all kinds of red flags started popping up outta nowhere. This girl lives at home with her moms, she has bad blood with her brother, but from this whip and her extravagant taste gives me the notion that this bitch is caked up. Or, was her parents caked up? The shit just wasn't adding up. I cut my eyes at her and thought; how old is this bitch? Ain't no way in hell I'm gonna get caught up and I ain't even got my feet wet yet.

Before she pulled off, I touched the steering wheel and said, "Look here Alisha, let's build for a second before we bounce." She sat back in her seat, already looking irritated from her mom's.

She crossed her arms then said, "What's up?"

"See Alisha" I'm the type of nigga that believe in a tit for tat. You scratch my back then I'm gonna scratch yours. 'It's something like the common courtesy system, feel me? If you remember while back I showed you my I.D and...

"So what, now you want to see mine?" She cracked up laughing then said, "Oh Puh-lease, you think I'm jail bait or something? I know your ass would hate to go back on a sex charge huh?" Her giggles transformed into mumbles while she opened her Prada wallet. She tossed it to me while she reversed the Camaro and said, "Here, I'm 22 years old, all legal. Anymore questions?"

As a matter fact, I did have a few more questions lingering, but I guess the one that was currently necessary would be the one that would connect the dots. It would shed some light on what I was working with, therefore I could play my cards right. With a quick exhale through my nose and with a polite verbal opposition, I asked her;

"What you do for a living?"

She looked at me with her eyes squinting, lit up with an inner glow of mischief, and then said, "I work that pole daddy, you ain't know?"

CHAPTER 4
KISMET

In a social context people of like minds are attracted to each other, which is the natural laws of attraction. It can only be understood in a universal plane of electromagnetism where like begets like. If you are negative then that's what you're going to attract, other negative niggas. Likewise, with positive. But if you are all out determined to win in a certain area or field, then all the tools, information and people you need in order to succeed will become accessible to you without breaking a sweat. it's like magic baby. The game is Real!

This is what makes life worth living. Believing in something and watching it manifest right before your eyes. In a nutshell, the laws of attraction and the game can be symbolized as my religion. I mean I'm just saying; call a spade a spade! If I was to pay attention to Sports center, studied the stats of athletes and was voluntarily glued to a television every Sunday, then sports would be my religion. If I knew Kim Kardashian, Paris Hilton and Miley Cyrus relationship status, can tell you Jay Z and Beyoncé's shorties name, never missed one episode of Empire, then celebrities and entertainment would be my religion.

For twelve long years, I worked hard for this position sitting next to this picture perfect dime piece. For twelve long years, I studied, planned ahead and was determined to be sitting right muthafucking here my dude. After all, living by the code means staying true to the game. Through Alisha's sunroof I took a glance at the heavens then silently said, "Thank you Game God."

Everything I'd been hoping for was coming to fruition but see, I'm not the one to count my chickens before they hatch so I had to test the waters, Does this position come with a fine print? What's the catch? Let me dig so I can find out.

While she was driving, I asked her, "So Alisha, how many shorties do you have?"

"Shorties?"

"Kids; how many kids you got?"

Alisha did a double take then said, "Baby, the last thing I need right now is some damn snotty nose kids running around. Please believe I do not have kids. What about you?"

"Nope" I said. "Never really thought about getting on that level and sitting my ass down to raise any. Parenthood is a full-time job, not part-time ya know?"

"Hmmmph, tell me about it."

Damn, I was pretty sure that would be it. Ah'ight fuck it, I can't be sitting up here playing this cat and mouse shit, so above all options, I gotta take it home, Do-Or-Die baby! While staring out the passenger's window looking at two black chicks walking down the street wearing cutoff shorts, bikini tops and flip-flops, I said, "You said that these Orange hoes are pretty messy right?"

"Oh yes indeed, don't say I didn't warn you."

She was giggling at her own statement while I shot back. "So you don't think they'll lace your man up that you got another nigga in the car?"

Alisha cracked up laughing, "My man? Oh my God no. I tried that and it only ended in a downward spiral. These niggas around here don't want nothing out of life. All they want to do is gang bang and smoke that wet shit. And besides, they stick they dick in everything moving and I personally do not have time for that. I'm just tryna stay on my grind. Until then, the right nigga is bound to pop up outta nowhere." She cut her eyes at me through the corner of her eyes then continued, "I work at Players in Beaumont because there's nothing here, and I mean nothing. My main priority right now is to get outta my mamma's house. I would shack up with my girl Maria but that crazy hoe be having way too many niggas coming in and out of there for free. And to be completely real with you, the only thing stopping me from moving out of my mamma's house right now today is because I don't want to live by myself. The world is getting crazier and crazier every day and I don't want to be feeling like no damn sitting duck just waiting on some lunatic to come disrupt my way of life. Can you feel where I'm corning from?"

I nodded yeah without interrupting her because I know the number one rule to any execution is to listen before action. Pay close attention to the wild kingdom and you will receive a clear understanding of how it works. A lion don't just run up on their prey and bum rush the attack at the first given sight. They carry out a more sinister approach by paying close attention to detail first by stalking their prey with calculated steps. Therefore, when it's time to execute, the prey has nowhere to run. People who do not understand this concept think it's about more talking; no nigga, it's about more listening. Especially if you already been chose.

Alisha gave me the run down about her background and pretty much her life story. It's a trip because after listening to her story, it became similar, if not identical to mine. She is originally from Las Cruces, New Mexico, where before she was born her mom's was an independent prostitute. Alisha came into the picture when a Mexican trick got her mom's pregnant then became overly obsessive to the degree of trying to kill her. Her mom's packed whatever she could carry then burnt off to Texas and landed in Orange.

Since then her mom's got saved and became a devout member of the First Baptist Church of Christ. She met Reverend Raymond Broussard who is originally a Louisiana coon ass but likewise, changed his life, and had a son with Alisha's moms soon after their enormous wedding ceremony. They are now putting a lot of pressure on Alisha with a ridiculous ultimatum; "Find another career or find somewhere else to live", which is contradictive because Alisha's brother is only 19 and he's already been to prison. Alisha says they treat her like Cinderella, like she's a bastard child or something because they do not apply the same pressure to her "in· and out of prison, lazy, unemployed, mentally unstable brother."

We finally pulled up to Alisha's crib located in a quiet residential area known as Roselawn. The house is far to the dead end curve of a street called Circle Q. All the houses in this neighborhood were pretty much traditional, clean with well-maintained front yards. There were no foreign whips parked in the driveways though. Only SUV's, soccer mom vans and a few RV's, which as a result gave me a clear understanding of where I was, "Familyville!"

"Be right back." Alisha said. "I'm gonna run in here and give this food to my momma, you gonna be ok?"

"Alisha I'm good, handle your business." I said while I watched her run towards the house.

I sat there waiting patiently while I tossed around the information that was automatically turning channels inside my dome. Now I'm laced with everything I need to know. That is unless later I'm surprised with some shit that I did not want to know. I mean I guess that's the facts of life. It's full of surprises and problems that initially wasn't a part of the plan. As of right now I only see one potential problem and he's standing outside on the front porch smoking a cigarette with an animated mask on his face. We stare at each other as if we're in a western showdown. Neither one of us broke our stare.

I even continued looking at the lil nigga when Alisha's car door opened. "Don't worry about him Threat, that boy ain't gonna bust a grape." As we pulled off, I threw Alisha's brother the duces but he only threw one finger back at me in return. Then he jacked his pants up from the crotch area.

I can see right now that this clown is a real live character.

Orange has two major streets, MacArthur and 16th street and as we were leaving Alisha's crib I noticed that these were the only two streets that had traffic lights. Alisha lives off MacArthur which has a line of car dealerships and fast food chains. Wendy's, Burger King, KFC; you know, the regulars. I also noticed a shopping center with a City trend right slap in the middle of that bitch and I couldn't help but laugh on the inside. I could only imagine everybody in this city shopping there, running around with the same gear on. Something from a scene from Coming To America when Eddie Murphey and Arsenio Hall's luggage was stolen. Then I peeped game that Walmart was the mega center, so they had not one but two places to shop for clothes.

My sister lives off 16th street, which caters to the convenience shopper. I see a Valero, a couple of liquor stores, Shop-N-Go, Dollar General and all that. But when I looked to the right pass Kroger's, I noticed off the top that down that way was the terrain of the hood. It's not that hard to figure out because I see a lime green, candy coated Oldsmobile cruising across a railroad track with at least 26 inch rims, sounding like a gorilla was trying to come out of the damn trunk. The nigga's shit was hitting hard because I could feel my heart flutter and he was at least fifty yards down the street. Alisha turned her head towards me and said, "We might be country but we definitely got slabs".

Alisha took me on a circle tour of Orange. She showed me the Oat Apartments, the projects and the Navy Edition, which is as she said, 'The Jungle of The Fruit'. Some of the houses were still vacant and boarded up due to Hurricane

Ike, Katrina and Rita, but the city has since then made restorations as to why you now see Mexicans in the city. She showed me the school where she graduated from (West Orange). She said Earl Thomas went to her school and from the day he was drafted into the NFL, everyone sidelined the Cowboy's and are now die hard Seattle Seahawk fans.

Around an hour later, we were right back where we started. We made a left on 17th street and entered yet another quiet residential neighborhood like Alisha's. Only difference, this one had a few foreign vehicles parked in the driveways. It was a little pass 2:00 PM when we finally pulled up to my sister's crib. A two story, Victorian style home with a gigantic ass tree in the middle of the front lawn. But dig, there was only one problem, and a big one at that. The front door stood behind an iron gate and the windows had security bars on them. No matter how fly its design, it still made the house look like a goddamn prison. Maya is most definitely gonna have to eighty-six that shit. No ifs, ands or buts about it.

Switching gears quick, I looked at Alisha then said, "Look, I appreciate the ride, hospitality and trust. You are the greatest. Don't know what I would have done without you. But check game. For the next week or two I'm gonna be hella busy so I'm gonna fall back into grind time. I believe we're on the same wavelength so you're familiar with what I'm stressing right?"

She nodded yeah so I asked her to toss me her phone. When she gave it to me I entered seven digits, saved it to her contacts under Threat and said, "Hit me no later than two weeks so we can catch up on introducing ourselves. I only gave you a first taste appetizer of the nigga before your eyes because believe me, there's a lot more to feast on." I can't call if she heard me or what because she was staring at her phone and contact dumbfounded. Nevertheless, the grimace look on her face was easy to read, so in a mello tone I said, "That's me Alisha."

"How the hell you got a phone already?"

I leaned in closer to her space then said "I have a lot of things Alisha."

"Well, how you know how to operate an IPhone and you been on lock for twelve years, tell me that?"

I politely took her visor cap off, and reached my hand to the back of her curly head. I brought her closer to me then I slowly kissed her forehead. I looked at her directly in the depths of her pretty eyes. I had her so close that she could actually feel the vibrations from my lips, I said, "And I know a lot of things Alisha!"

Her eyes were closed and her mouth was partially open so it was crystal clear that she was expecting me to put my tongue down her throat. Instead I said, "I guarantee you that the next time you see me, things will be a lot different."

She slowly opened her eyes then said, "I feel that."

All of a sudden she quickly rose up with buck shot eyes and equal sized grin. She started waving her hand rapidly and was making eye contact with someone, only it wasn't with me. I twisted my body so fast I thought my rib snapped. When I turned around I see my sister Maya walking towards the Camaro with sparkling eyes and a peaceful smile with her arms wide open.

CHAPTER 5
SURPRISE KING

One thing we do as humans, when we meet people for the first time we start scanning their faces for their strengths and weaknesses, for the lights and scars that will tell us something about who they are and where they been. But see, Maya has no physical flaws; you know, the bent nose, crooked teeth or cocked eye we would normally use as a signifier? No sir, I'm proud to say that my sister is proper and that over the past twelve years she's grown into one hellava woman. When she walks into any room, niggas start walking into furniture.

Maya is smart, pretty and even a little goofy at the same time. Mostly she's compared to Keri Hilson. Both are beautiful, tall, same caramel skin and sport similar hair styles. I was tripping when she first cut her hair but after a couple of visits I got use to the fit. When Halle Berry and Toni Braxton first hit the scene it was like the green light for all pretty chicks to start chopping their hair off. Every since then it's been a goddamn epidemic, Maya stands at 5'11 so we stand almost eye to eye, but to the average female she's hovering over them with a slight intimidation, I mean to the one that's packing that insecure shit anyway because her relaxed smile draws people closer. Right now she's casually dressed in khaki capris, brown sandals showing her toes painted in a pale coral and she's wearing a white T-shirt with GOT CARS written on the front. When I opened Alisha's car door with my red chain bag resting on my shoulder, I stood tall with my shoulders back, chest out, chin high.

Maya said, "Look at you, get over here and give me a hug."

Her arms were still stretched wide open as if she wanted to hug the entire world but now her hands were expeditiously opening and closing, suggesting for me to get my ass over there.

Now, I've hugged my sister several times over the years at visitation but it was something significantly different about this one. As I embraced my sister I noticed the small things that I never experienced before. The humming in my ear, her shaky hands wrapped around my shoulders and the drumming of her feet. I felt the genuine love and embrace that only siblings know about. That real shit!

"Oh my God Threat, it's finally over." Maya said as she stood back for another look.

While I was closing Alisha's car door I said, "No, no sis, it just begun.

Alisha leaned closer to the passenger's window then said, "Girl, he's been a complete gentleman."

"Yeah, he can be a real sweetheart. Thanks by the

way." Maya said to Alisha with a thumb up. When Alisha returned the thumbs up, including a winking eye, I figured it was some type of secret code that women or only these two women knew about. But I didn't call it into question; I just gave Alisha a two finger salute when she drove off. Alisha honked her horn twice then seconds later I heard the thumping beat of Rihanna fading down the once before quiet street.

"She's something else." Maya said while sympathetically shaking her head but still with a smile that said it was all good. Anyway, completely changing the subject, she asked me, "So these are the clothes they give you when you're released? A job wouldn't happen to come with the shirt, now would it? 'Pablo'?"

She giggled at her own sarcasm while she dragged my arm towards the house. The hot sun was beaming down hard and it didn't show any sign of letting up. So I made a sun visor of my hand and followed Maya while she led the way.

"This iron gate and the bars on the window are gonna have to go sis. No more locked doors." I said mimicking the dude from the Friday movie. Sounding corny as hell I know but at the same time I was serious as cancer. I closed both doors behind us as we were entering her humble abode, she said, "Well for one, the insurance policy won't allow it. I can do renovations but not with security. There's this thing called The Home Owner's Association and they go around telling people what they can and can't do to their own property."

"What's the consequence? I asked her while looking

around her crib, mesmerized by my sister's quality of taste.

"More than likely a big fat fine."

"Then we'll pay it."

She put her hands on her hips then said, "Money can't buy everything Threat."

"Yeah, well I like to see you live without it." I said while flopping back on her custom sofa with the extra-large throw pillows.

I tossed my red chain bag to the side while I scoped out the art on the walls, many by me. Her living room has a two story ceiling, a fireplace and an entertainment center with a wide screen Samsung curved UHD TV resting in the front. She was watching a recorded episode of Orange is The New Black. I noticed on her glass coffee table around six different food menu selections but I wanted to stick to the subject at hand, so I said, "I deeply apologize for starting our reunion off on a negative note, I mean if that's what you want to call it, but as your older brother I'm telling you that the bars on the front door and the windows has to go. It's non-negotiable so please don't make a big deal out of this Maya."

"Oh my lord; what's the deal with you and the damn bars? You're not in prison anymore Threat, it's over, you're free, and the bars don't even matter."

I felt my muscles clenching along my jaw line, which I guess is why I was talking through gritted teeth. Leaning in with my elbows on my knees, I said, "I'm not concerned or even thinking about me, this is about you Maya."

"Me?" She asked with her hand to her chest.

"Yeah you! How you think them muthafuckers killed

moms and dad? The bars Maya! They trapped them in by locking the bars with a lock and chain. What you forgot?"

Maya cocked her head to the side with an unhurried walk to the sofa. She slouched in then said, "Oh, right that."

She closed her eyes, I'm guessing to clearly recall the memory. We were only in elementary school but still to this day the memory remains live and vivid as if it were in HD. She pressed her lips together then shook her head as if she were trying to erase the negative Image from her mind. She stood up quick and said "Okay, okay, I get it. I will do what I can about the bars but what I'm not about to do is sit up here and be depressed on my brother's reunion. Do you understand me?" She was fighting back her tears, although one slipped down, she still managed to uphold that genuine smile on her face. "Rumor has it that someone was intending to surprise me today?" She said as she wiped the tear and sniffed her nose.

"Who me?" I asked as if I didn't know what she was talking about.

"MmHm, well if you didn't know that I am the surprise king around here then you will soon find out."

"Oh really?"

"Yes really! I got your voice message while I was at work and right before I was about to start panicking, your new friend texted me this."

She walked over to me and made sure I seen the text with my own two eyes. It said: I HAVE THREAT SO U DON'T HAVE 2 RUSH. WILL DROP HIM OFF @ YOUR HOUSE @ AROUND 2. OMG HE"S CUTE. PUT

A GOOD WORD IN FOR YA GIRL. LMAO,!!!!

As she was walking towards the kitchen she said, "So you were released a day early huh?"

"Oh you didn't get the memo?" I asked her, displaying my wide grin.

"No I didn't get the memo, but what I did get is your favorite Chinese takeout." She said with triumph in her eyes.

She returned to the living room carrying a large platter with several cartons of Chinese food. I didn't play around; I rolled my sleeves up and dug in. Chinese food? Man, nigga I been waiting on this for over a decade and she's right, it's my favorite. But what she also knows is that the best route to win any nigga's heart is through the stomach. I chowed down on Moo Shu Pork, Szechuan Beef, Pot Stickers, and Egg Fu young and smashed a carton of fried rice, while she spooned up a hot and sour soup with a side of hot shrimp with Chinese broccoli.

We kicked it, laughed, reminisced and enjoyed each other's company. We even had desert and went hard on a bowl of salted caramel ice cream. But the surprises were far from over. Maya popped a disk inside the DVD player and I was at the edge of the couch when I seen that it was a documentary about my old man. Double T, the greatest pimp of the Mid West had brilliant ideas and took the game to another level. The documentary showed his accomplishments and stables throughout Chicago, Milwaukee, Detroit and Cincinnati. It went into detail about an organization he started titled I.C.C.P.P.P (International, Cross, Country, Professional, Paid, Pimpin) and praised him as an internationally known pimp and genius of his era. It also showed his transition to square up with my mom's but to this day their murders still stand as a cold case.

Maya and I stayed together, even at the foster home. When I turned 18 I copped an apartment on the south side of Minneapolis, so by the time Maya was released we were straight. When I went to prison in 2003 was considered our first separation so you know, today is not only a reunion but it's also a celebration. Celebrating the evidential fact that no matter what we seen or been through, we will remain bonded together not only like siblings but as if we were inseparable Siamese twins.

Maya escorted me upstairs to the guest room, which I already know is going to be my temporary spot. She can actually get into interior design as a side gig because the space asserts my personality. It's masculine with brown and white stripped walls, a media/library, hardwood flooring with a solid black wool rug, a black Inmod ball chair and a brown and white linen upholstered bed. Catty cornered to the window sits a small wooden desk with everything I needed resting on the top. Maya walked over to the desk then said, "This laptop might be a bit slow because the only one I could find on sale was at a pawnshop, so yeah, it might be very slow. But this tablet is hair trigger fast. Now, right here is the 94 Lg smart phone so if you need an internet back up then this little sucker got you covered. In the box is one thousand business cards with your name, website, email, phone contact and title: Professional Artist. Behind the door is the closet and in there you'll find all the clothes you requested from every shoe to every thread; it's all there. Everything just as you ordered, Mr. Threat!"

Maya has been the perfect muscle for me over the years. I don't care what kind of ambitions, passions or great ideas you have while you're in prison, if you don't have the muscle in the 'Free World' to promote that shit then it's just a mere fantasy. But this pawnshop shit got me twisted. I rather have second hand shoes then second hand technology. But hey, I guess even your muscles cramp up every now and then. I opened the laptop for my own investigation to peep it's quality and speed because if it's too slow then I wouldn't need it. When the laptop powered on, my eyebrows raised at the first sight of the screen saver. It was a nigga dressed in military fatigue, sitting on the hood of a Humvee, obviously in another country with an M16 in his hand.

"Now I don't know what you think I'm into" I said to Maya, "But this shit right here most definitely ain't it." When I turned around, Maya was rubbing the back of her neck with her chin dipped into her chest.

She cleared her throat then said, "I thought I deleted that after I sent and pasted it to my desktop, sorry."

I turned around to get a better look at the picture to see if I knew him because it could possibly be someone we knew back home. When I came to the realization that I never seen him before in my life, I asked Maya, "Who is this nigga anyway?"

"Um, that's Edwin", "Edwin who?"

"Edwin Walters."

"Maya, you know what I mean. Where you know him from?"

"Well, I was meaning to tell you about that. See, what had happen was, Maya cracked up laughing, I'm guessing to ease the tension but I was still staring at her anticipating a response. "Seriously though" Maya said, "Me and Edwin been talking for around two years now. He's deployed in Afghanistan so as of right now all we do is chat online."

Maya whips out her phone, showing me a picture that this nigga Edwin posted on Instagram. It was a picture of him skydiving while intending to land on a large message that was engraved in the sand, it said: MAYA I LOVE YOU!

"This is just one example of how much he goes out of his way to prove his love for me." Maya said, "We're good Threat, I mean no weird energy, nothing." Maya was rubbing her hands down her shorts with a lot of goddamn blinking. She's waiting on me to say something, anything I guess, but why is she so nervous all of a sudden? I think I know why.

While I was closing the laptop I said, "I just want to ask you one question and I don't need you lying to me either."

"I'm listening."

I faced Maya with my arms crossed and my head deliberately lowered so I could study her body language. Inhaling deep to be sure I kept my composure. I asked her, "Did you meet this nigga online?"

I must have ignited something deep within because her nervousness changed to a sudden blast of ghetto attitude. She threw her hands up in the air and said; "Uh uh, see, I knew you was gonna go there Threat, I just knew it. But don't come up in here trying to judge me because I don't judge you. Yes, I met him online okay! But now that this is out in the open you should know that the University of Google is where I got my degree, so please believe that I'm going to look some stuff up on whoever comes my way. Besides, I know how to social network; I'm not one of them selfie addicts whose brains don't work and always quick to blog, link or tweet. Or one of them perverts who post pics of their ass or genitals all day. I got this Threat; seriously, Edwin and I are on the same page. I mean he's not like on my profile or anything like that, what I meant is level, we are on the same level, you know what I'm trying to say right?"

I most definitely knew what she was trying to say. That her mind was trapped inside the World Wide Web, just like the whole wide world. The internet is a vast international communication system and a repository of information offered to any and every one with internet access. It is offered to the public because the public has an insatiable curiosity to know shit about any and everything, except what's worth knowing. My sister is caught up in a trend of virtual fantasy where in that 'fantasy' you can be anybody and anything you wanted to be. It offers entertainment, employment, comfort, drama, information and you already know...Romance! Sorry to say but the internet is my baby sister's religion.

Although fantasy sometimes is better than reality especially if it makes you happy. Right then I understood that I couldn't judge her. If she likes it then I love it. But one thing she will have to understand is that as long as she's enjoying it, then my life and freedom will be in constant jeopardy. If someone so far as thinks to hurt Maya physically, mentally or any other kind of way then I will never see daylight again.

But check it, I already applied a lot of pressure to Maya and I don't plan on maxing her out with stress in the first couple hours of my release, so I'm gonna let bygones be bygones and fall back. I will temporary accept this computer love bull-shit and face the fact that I can't control my little sister's life.

It is what it is, feel me? So I sucked it up, swallowed hard and said, "Yeah, I know what you mean Maya, I was just asking. That's what's up!"

Her mouth fell open with a slight tilt in her head, "You mean you're not mad?"

"Mad, why would I be mad? Your life is your life. But you need to know that if he hurts you then... No Maya, I'm good."

Maya pretended to faint; she fell back on the bed then Immediately hopped back up with glow in her eyes. She rubbed her hands together then said, "Okay that's great because I have something else to show and tell you."

While we were walking down stairs I snapped to the cold hard fact that I just got played. My sister is on some other shit no doubt. There was once upon a time she didn't dream of challenging me, much less play me. I think she planned this shit all the way down to a science and went out of her way to set this whole stage up and ya man is the star. I fell for the okeydoke. The laptop is slow bullshit. More like the laptop is bait. She knows damn well that I can't operate any productive business on a slow or low quality laptop, therefore it was a grand invention so we could get this subject outta the way.

I was introduced to an episode of let's make a deal. Door number one; accept it and we can keep moving on with your surprises. Door number two, don't accept it; then your surprises end here. I just received one of the most sinister ultimatums that anyone could Imagine by my own flesh 'n blood. What in the hell is this world coming to? I was lead to the kitchen, which was another space that was designed with an artistic eye. Fresh dark wood, custom white lacquer cabinetry, limestone floors with porcelain countertops, including the island. You could see a casual but stylish breakfast room from the kitchen but for some reason it looks as if it's only for show. See what we can do about that I thought.

I sat down on one of the stools to the island and said, "Maya, this kitchen is fly, what's up is this your work?"

"Yeah, pretty much." She said while opening the stainless steel refrigerator. "This kitchen was built from scratch. When I first got the place it looked like something straight from the 70's with outrageous colors. So I thought a more modern look would give it a Maya's touch." She said giggling. She slid me a cold fizzy mineral water and said, "Even this porcelain countertop causes stares coming from people in this town. But see, people are moving towards quartz or porcelain countertops these days because they're thin and extremely durable. That's why it's Important to keep up with the times or else you would be staring at yellow wallpaper with bluebonnet flowers right now."

I raised my eyebrows, and then she said, "Yeah I know; scary!"

She sat down on the opposite side of the island countertop then continued. Only now her mood has quickly changed to something a little bit more serious. With strong eye contact and a steady low pitched voice she said. "While back I was listening to a song on the radio and the beginning words was something like: There are two things in life that are constant, that's change and change. Now that makes so much sense on all sorts of levels. For one, the world around us evolves and constantly changes every day and every season, so do people. But we as people get caught up in trying to change other people into our liking, and that doesn't make any sense to me. A person is gonna do them regardless of what anyone else considers to be right or wrong. It's just human nature you know?"

Maya gently bit her bottom lip and locked her hands together to force a calm and stillness. She looked as if she was preparing herself for the best case scenario. Her breath was temporarily bottled up in her chest and as she released it she said, "Now Threat, there are so many things that I think you should be doing. For instance, I think you should focus on your art and writing, in the meantime find a part time job. Your potentials are endless; I mean you did the unimaginable. Everything from that perfect and fast laptop, by the way, to the clothes in the closet up there you paid for with your own money you made all from a jail cell. Just Imagine what you could do out here? I been stressing about this for a while, until I finally said; you know what? I can't do this! I have to let go and let Threat be who he is."

Maya put her head down and went quiet with closed eyes. When she opened them she looked up towards the ceiling then took a deep, pained breath, she said "Yes I know who you are Threat and yes I know what you're going to do. You have to understand that we are both apples from the same tree so I know what's in your blood. Can I change that? I hardly doubt it. You have a lot of passion in your heart and I know where it comes from. From the guys that snitched on you who were supposed to be your friends, all the way to the death of our parents. You have something to prove and nothing not even me is going to stop you. So I rather be with you then against you. I love you Threat and only God knows that I don't want to lose you. But if it's a pimp you want to be, then be the best fucking one this world has ever seen." Maya reached in her pocket then slid me a pair of car keys with a Cadillac emblem on a small gold chain then said "I think you're going to need this!"

I sat there with a blank stare with the keys in hand. Maya twisted my wig back would be a meager description of how I felt. She deserved a round of applause for her performance today. She is a true artist, gifted and crafted with creativity. She's right; we come from the same tree so it shouldn't be no surprise that my sister would come hard or not come at all.

Maya's grand finale was introduced when she opened the garage door from the kitchen. I was greeted with a silver 2015 Cadillac CTS. The lights coming from the ceiling made the lac look as if it were on the show room floor. But Maya stole the show when she gave me an orientation, sounding like the car sales woman that she is. Walking around the car in controlled strides, she said, "Threat, this car is just like you. handsome and very powerful. The Cadillac CTS V Sport sedan fits you to a T. It starts with a powerful motor, an all-new 420 horsepower, twin turbocharged V6, a new eight speed automatic transmission. Inside it's smart like you too because it has a multimedia system with GPS, a 14 inch smart touchscreen controlled by an IDrive like knob and a touch pad that deciphers characters drawn with your fingertip. Black leather diamond stitched interior and the surround sound system is powered by Bose. The body is a perfect match with yours. It has a sexy silver paint that shines even at night. A strong aerodynamic appearance with a custom chrome mesh two part grille. This huge moon roof will invite you to the stars where you belong and the 18 inch chrome wheels will cap everything off. Now I had to pull a few strings to make this happen but your invoices from your art and book sales, with the already existing account pretty much did all the hard work. Did you know that your credit score is higher than mine? I shouldn't be saying that out loud but hey, it's the truth. We will finance the car through your bank or whatever works best for you, okay? You will be able to afford payments, right?"

My expression on my face must have spoken out loud because she said, "Sorry, dumb question."

CHAPTER 6
"THE GAME IS TO SOLD NOT TOLD"

Friday morning started with a ten mile run to Bridge City and back. At 4:45AM I was crossing the Rainbow Bridge. At 6:38AM I was in the kitchen cooking Maya breakfast. I cooked her an omelet with ham and cheese, bell peppers, hash browns, sliced tomatoes, buttered biscuits and orange juice with pulp. She walked in the kitchen yawning because the morning breakfast aroma woke her up twenty two minutes prior to her actual alarm sound off. She was surprised to see the breakfast room occupied with plates, glasses, a pitcher of orange juice and food. I mean the regular shit that constitutes a breakfast room, right?

Would you call a bathroom a bathroom without a toilet and shit paper? Hell no because a bathroom is to use, not for show. One thing that is for show is the CNN morning news because it's most definitely not to inform. At 8:00AM while Maya went to work I watched mainstream news with biting criticism and an increased blood flow straight to the eye sockets. Every news channel they're shoving bullshit down your throat that don't matter to anything unless you're into useless actions of violence, racism, celebrity gossip or the whereabouts of Hillary Clinton's emails. Nothing on inflation or unemployment rates, index of stock, factors of production like land, labor or capital. You know, the shit that matters?

The mainstream media controls the mentality and actions of its viewers. It's to the point now that as long as most Americans could have their fast food drive through, listen to their IPods, play with their cell phones, gossip on Facebook and watch American Idol then they could care less about what's actually going on in their country. Bread and Circus! The Romans had it right; as long as people had food and fun then they could care less about the erosion of their nation.

My mind was set in that political science, government conscious state that comes with lack of sleep. Maybe that's the reason why I've been periodically hearing voices again. All I hear is my name being called, but I haven't carried out a formal diagnosis because as of right now, it's like I said, due to lack of sleep. I have been up majority of the night trying to retrace my steps over the past twelve years. The question at hand; how in the hell did Maya know my intentions? A pimp? Where and how did she do the math to come up with that?

After reading my 'Critical Study List' I could see why. I ordered books on everything from Manipulations and Mind Control, Sexual Perversions of The Rich and Wealthy, The Real Casanova, to The Art of Seduction. My Critical Study List shows my interest in subjects like The Stockholm Syndrome, Wit and Charm, The History of White Slavery, all the way to Scouting Techniques. But what really took it home I think was my obsession with psychology; after all, it's my major. I'm a few credits shy of receiving my masters in psychology. But here's the hook; I don't have any plans on becoming a psychologist. So anybody with a rational thinking mind can put two and two together and peep that I plan to resurrect what's in my blood, especially if we share the same type.

Yeah, Maya's blood type is a lot similar to mine than you actually realize because I think she has a little sumpin, sumpin sinister going down herself. I haven't put my finger on it yet but I'm not buying that she bought a home, manages a home and is currently doing renovations on a home, all on a car sales commission. She said that she shouldn't be saying it out loud but my credit score is higher than hers. Well then how in the hell are you paying for the shit Maya? Right then I thought of Niccolo Machiavelli and what he quoted in The Prince: "It is very necessary to appear to have them. And I shall dare to say this also, that to have them and always to observe them is injurious, and that to appear to have them is useful; to appear merciful, faithful, humane, religious, upright, and to be so, but with a mind so framed that should you require not to be so, you may be able and know how to change to the opposite."

Maya's practicing my own game. Is she using the shit against me? Is she trying to show me that she's smarter than me? Let me take my ass to sleep before I drive myself insane.

Saturday we celebrated Independence Day with her car selling colleagues. Three middle aged white women, a

Mexican lady around thirtyish and two niggas who could pass for distant kin. I fired up the grill, we laughed, played a game of spades while their kids argued about who had next on slip 'n slide. Everything was cool and copacetic until I became the center of concern.

"What was it like in prison? Did you ever get lonely? What are you going to do now that you're out? Have you considered selling cars?"

Damn, they hit me with the 50 Cent 21 question hot track, but only this track was set on replay. Maya peeped my irritation which is why she didn't say shit when I skipped out. I found myself chilling with the kids where they kicked my ass on the PlayStation they brought with them. Mind you, these were seven and eight year old kids. Hey nigga don't hate, these shorties today are advanced.

Sunday I used Maya's SUV to get familiar behind the wheel again. I even hit I-10 and drove to Beaumont and back. I practiced parallel parking, school zone speeds, signals, sign identifications and all that. Monday morning Maya took me to the OMV and I aced both written and driving test. The same day.

I went to my bank (Capital One) and finally introduced myself to the manager. I opened another checking, savings, automobile financing and a business expansion account. They tossed me a debit and two credit cards because I was considered a credit worthy customer.

My first art sales in prison were direct deposited into my account Maya started for me with $50.00. By the time I was able to maintain a balance of $1,500.00 I had the ability to borrow to raise funds. I borrowed money only to pay the interest back. When I knocked off another project it was straight up to pay the interest, that's it. I been with the same contract with AT&T for over eight years where I paid the cell phone bill with the account name Thomas Threat. I bought appliances, jewelry and small stocks only to put it up for collateral. So all the money I played with over the years was for one reason and one reason only: To upgrade my credit.

I couldn't have done none of this shit without my muscle, Maya. The money on my TDCJ account basically came from book sales. I wrote three published books, a stage play and an umpteen number of poems. My first book was hard to get out there because I didn't know the game. I spent my wheels trying to find an agent whereas the muthafucka expected me to pay a publishing cost.

Sometimes an agent can be just as ruthless as a lawyer because he wanted me to pay an additional copying, messenger, and an express mail fee. It didn't stop there; he even wanted me to pay him a reading fee just to evaluate my manuscript. I thought to myself, fuck an agent. I went straight to the source and became my own agent. Submitting to a publisher is the same as submitting to an agent. I had Maya buy a manuscript box from Office Depot; she slapped a cover page on it then mailed it straight to the publisher. Next thing you know I get a letter from the publisher saying that they want to publish my book and that they would seal the deal with a $5,000.00 advancement check. Did I accept the check? Hell no! The letter itself was more important because it was proof and my validated credential that there was a publisher willing to publish my book. I rolled the dice and mailed the letter to the agent, showing him that there was a publisher willing to get at me. Then presto, just like magic the agent fucked with me without additional fees and helped me get a $15,000.00 advancement.

My book, The Art of Doing Time became a saleable item in bookstores, Amazon and eBooks. It was a hot commodity because there were women across the U.S. sending their nigga's the book, encouraging them to get on my level. An A to Z format on how to take advantage of prison and how to come out winning. It's an illuminating guide that gives detailed and clear explanations on how to build a craft, refuse the common everyday bullshit and it provides brilliant examples on how to knock on the door to greatness.

After "The Art of Doing Time," I didn't have a problem getting my next two books published because I developed a name. Once you get a name, it's like Gucci baby, the shit's gonna sell regardless of the content. How you think Robert Greene became so successful after the 48 Laws of Power? The game is to be sold not told.

Tuesday I got the lac registered and insured. I paid a five year premium for a full coverage policy. Then I studied and mastered the multimedia system and GPS. I figured out how to use the touchscreen radio by downloading music and a couple of Apps. I now have UBER and HOT SPOT LOCATERS. There's nothing here in Orange except a bar named Spanky's and a hole in the wall club called DJ's but Beaumont is popping with strip clubs, good restaurants, a mall and a slew of furniture outlets.

One week later to the exact, I got a special delivery from the post office. After I signed for it, a check for sixty stacks was finally in my possession. However not for long though because I drove straight to the bank and deposited the whole check, leaving me with no cash but with a pocket full of loaded plastic and A1 credit. The following day I drove to Houston and dropped ten stacks on the best Criminal Law attorney in the south and northern Texas regions. George Bertolucci, an Italian who has his own firm now represents me just in case of an emergency. I will drop stacks on him every month like clockwork because having a lawyer in your corner is the cornerstone of all investments. You can't predict the future so it's like insurance. "Are you in good hands?"

On the way back from Houston I stopped at the Parkdale Mall and slid my card for a couple threads, a wavelength taper fade, some wrist wear and a link so I could be official. When Maya came home from work she tossed her keys on the kitchen's island, opened the refrigerator then said, "Hey that girl came by my office said she's been trying to contact you."

"Who?"

"Alisha!"

Maya gave me a piece of paper with a number written on it then said, "Here, I wrote her number down from my phone. I think it would be in your best interest to call her back. I hear she's real talented up there on that stage." Maya winked her eye at me then giggled her way to her bedroom.

CHAPTER 7
THE COURTSHIP

It was moments before dark when I finally hit Alisha from my cell. I was playing the stall game. I wanted to shake things up a little by turning off my phone at the very exact time frame that I told her to get at me. This way I would be able to peep her mental stability. Would she pop up at the scene unannounced? Would she blow my phone up franticly because she couldn't contact me? Either way I would have wrote her off as a crazy bitch.

Using my sister as a mediator tells me that she at least has common sense. But see, although I was playing the stall game I still knew not to burn a potential bridge because this could work either way. She could easily write me off as a nigga who's all talk.

"What's up Threat? I called you when you said but your phone was going straight to voice mail." Alisha said when she answered my call.

I didn't explain why the phone was off or come up with an extravagant lie, I just asked her, "How you holding up, you good?"

She exhaled through the phone, "Well you know, as good as can be expected. I have to get outta this house before I lose it. My retarded ass brother is working with my nerves, oh my God, I wish he would poof and be gone. And my momma and her husband is just as bad because I will never be the goody two shoes they expect me to be, and I sho ain't about to fake the funk."

"What you doing now?" I asked her while I was peeping the time from my laptop.

It was 7:15 when she said, "I'm about to go to work. Wednesday night's nothing but high rollers be coming to the club."

Right then at that split second, at that exact time I realized I was ready. It was now or never, do or die, mildew or barbeque. So I said, "Alright get ready, I'm going with you."

I disconnected the line, leaving no options to disagree. The world is about to get a double dose of me. I am what I am and what I am not I will never be. Like the Minnesota winters, I'm cold as ice. Like the Chicago wind, I'm unstoppable. The game is real and it's pretty evident that it chose me to represent it. I was destined to walk this path ever since my creation, because I was born a pimp by blood and most definitely not by relation. I hopped in the shower and came out feeling live and brand new. After drying myself off and putting on fresh scented Clarins Men's antiperspirant, I opened the closet and knew exactly what I was going to wear. Looking good from the inside out is the hook. Your body, your threads, your swag, your talents, all the way to the words that come out of your mouth is the hook that's going to reel something in, moreover the bait that gets any player chose.

I put on a pair of black Tom Ford slacks, a Ralph Lauren Black Label three button Polo shirt with a black Paul Smith slim fit wool blend suit jacket. On my feet I wore black Italian Oxford shoes with a black soft leather Gucci belt. I put on two eight carat crushed offset diamond earrings, one white gold link around my neck and an Oyster Perpetual Sky Dweller Rolex watch on my wrist. While I examined my work in the bathroom mirror I was reassured beyond any doubt that I was ready. My golden skin is glistening with glow, my pearly whites are shining, my taper fade is perfect with a throw back Steve Harvey edge up and my mustache and beard is razor sharp with a chin strap trim. I put on my Giorgio Armani, coca cola tint frames, put ten business cards inside my wallet, sprayed three shots of Nautica Life, popped two mints, then said, "This shit ain't no optical illusion, I see a muthafucking pimp, and the world is about to witness one too."

I opened the garage door then sat peacefully inside the CTS with my eyes closed and my head tipped back. Taking in a deep satisfied breath, the smell circulating from the leather mixed with the new interior smelt intoxicating. Damn this car is sexy! I thought as I opened the sun roof, turned on the A/C, and then searched the touchscreen for downloaded songs. While I had the CTS in reverse, backing out slowly, Fat Pat came through the surround sound, "25 lighters on my dresser, yes sir, I gets to get paid, I got 25 lighters on my dresser."

Driving down 16th street heads turn and bounce in my direction. It was now dark and the moon was in full bloom. The moon appeared larger than normal and glowed as if it were a spotlight, fulfilling an obligation to shine down strictly on me. I even felt like the stars above were watching me through the sun roof because I saw one twinkle as soon as I glanced up. Or maybe it was just the Game God giving me a winking eye that my intentions were moving in the right direction. Seconds before I reached MacArthur, my phone lit up.

"What's up Alisha?" I said answering the call.

There was a brief silence on the line before she said "I was wondering if you wanted me to pick you up, I'm about to leave in a few minutes."

"No!" I said, "Just be outside, I'll be there in a five minutes."

I disconnected the line again before she asked a third degree of questions. I knew she was fishing but I had to keep her guessing. She was more than likely wondering how I was going to get there, if I'm with anyone and if I knew my way to her crib. One thing I was blessed with is a photographic memory. You will never have to tell me the same shit twice and if I been somewhere once then please understand that I know how to get there again. I even studied the route to Players because how in the hell are you going to be an effective, anything for that matter if you have to ask a bitch for directions? Same thing applies to people who always depend on GPS.

I see Alisha outside when I pulled up to her house; I parked next to the curb. She had on a pink and white jumpsuit, white leather Coach Sneakers with a solid pink backpack. She didn't have on a hat this time nor was her hair in a ponytail so you could see the full length of her thick natural curly hair. She was squatting and squinting, trying her hardest to see who, or if it was me behind the tint. While she was still looking through the window, now with her hands positioned to the side of her face as if it was going to help her see better. I pressed the button so the passenger's window could roll down. When it was all the way down, I helped her out.

I said, "It's me Alisha, get in."

Alisha stood there with her palms up as if she were waiting on me to explain how this picture was possible.

When I didn't say shit she said, "This nigga right here."

With a playful grin and shaking her head at the same time. When she opened the door she tossed her backpack to the backseat and said, "Damn, what you do, win the lottery or something?"

Before I could respond, she already had her phone out taking a picture of me. I didn't stop her, how could I? Besides, the picture had significance. At least she was proud to be sitting next to this Boss Player right now. But still, there were limitations. As I pulled off I said, "Don't post that picture Alisha."

"Oh trust, I'm far from stupid, I know what's up. This picture is for me with your sexy ass."

Before we approached the ramp to I-10 I asked her if she wanted anything from the store while I fuel up. I wanted to knock off a box of condoms anyway so I needed a reason to stop. She said, "Damn, you musta read my mind. A couple of energy drinks would be cool. They be trying to deduct our tips for their watered down ass drinks and I really don't have any plans on going off on anyone tonight."

We were parked at the fuel pump at Vallero's to the right of the service road. Before I got out, I leaned closer to Alisha with strong eye contact, I said, "I want to ask you something but I need you to be real with me no matter what you might think the outcome might be for being straight up."

"What's up, keeping it real ain't hard to do?"

"Ah'ight, check game" I said, "Over the past two weeks did you ever google my name; you know, investigating who I am?"

"Daddy, one way or another you're gonna come to the conclusion that I ain't some lunatic bitch. I don't get down like all these messy Orange hoes around here who don't have anything better to do but play detective. It's plain and simple, if you want me to know something about you, you'll tell me right?"

"True that!" I said, and you will soon know everything you need to know, but to start this off right, first you need to know who I was in prison. I opened my wallet then gave her one of my business cards. I said, "While I go in here I want you to look at this webpage and it will pretty much sum up what kind of level I been on for the past twelve years.

Alisha didn't waste any time searching the website from her phone, which reassured me that she never seen the shit. Right before I opened the door to the Valero I turned around and seen Alisha look up from her phone. Maybe because the page was still buffering, who knows? All I know is that she was staring at me with a silly grin and smiling pretty much at nothing. I could read her lips from where I stood. She said, "Sexy ass!"

See, I'm in the process of a courtship right now. If you pay attention to a peacock and notice the male peacock has a train of up to 150 tail feathers, which can be erected in display to form a fan that he loves to show off. When he's in the process of a courtship he uses it to his advantage. When he's trying to get chose he spreads his feathers as far as they could possibly go with his chest out. Birds do a fly dance, gorilla's pound on their chest, lions roar as loud as they can and so on. But see, right now I'm doing it with my talents. It's an effective hook that places you in an elite category and if you have other hooks to go with it, then the bitch has no other choice but to follow suit.

Also I'm in the middle of a construction. In any construction, whether it's a skyscraper, a house or in the game of pimping, you have to start from the bottom. The bottom is the foundation which in fact keeps everything grounded. Without a solid foundation everything else will crumble. Alisha fits the criteria of a bottom bitch where instinctively she already knows her position. She could be the winning combination of her black and Mexican lineage, making her the exotic prototype that was necessary for every pimp. She symbolizes my arrival to the top because she could unmistakably be with any nigga she fixed her trance inducing eyes on. And when she finally chooses me, then it's going to place me in the league with Caesar: "I came; I saw; I conquered!" Which I should be able to lock her without a sweat because I feel that she's already convinced that I ain't the average Joe Blow.

The lac was now sitting on a full tank. According to the code, me pumping gas is a sin punishable by death. Especially with the quality of gear I have on right now. But it's just like a construction; you have to start from the bottom up, so your hands will experience a little dirt in the process. As soon as I opened the door I gave Alisha her energy drinks, I put the condoms in my pocket, and said, "So what you think?"

"Oh my God, are you serious? You have skills...I never would have guessed this." She showed me a chalk drawing I did of Pimp C as if I never seen the shit before. "Look at this one of Pimp C." You have no idea, I just love me some Pimp C."

"I seen that one." I said while she laughed and kept repeating. "This is amazing. This is so fucking amazing." She said, "And you wrote three books and a play? Oh trust, I will be ordering a copy tonight."

I wanted to slow her down a little bit because I was about to, out of the blue switch gears without a warning. I took a glance at her and she was still staring at her phone with raised eyebrows. While I was entering the ramp to I-10 I reached for her phone then politely placed it upside down on her lap, and said, "Alisha, fuck that and dig this. Let's build for a minute."

She crossed her arms with a still demeanor then said, "What's up?"

Diverting my attention back and forth from the

highway and Alisha's eyes, I said, "Look here Alisha; there are a few more important brass tacks that you need to know about me before we can press forward. Number one principal is important that you clearly understand that I don't believe in gimmicks or going to play you with tricks. Meaning, I'm going to put everything on the table right there for you to look at, feel me? You can analyze it, quiz it, examine it; whatever you like for whatever it's worth. If you reject it then cool, no hard feelings, we can keep it moving and go about our separate ways. But if you accept it then it would be the best..."

"Get to the point Threat." Alisha said, still with her arms crossed, except now she was gazing at the stars through the sunroof. Now this type of response would have intimidated the average simp nigga, but it only boosted a real nigga's ego.

I said, "I'm a pimp Alisha! Hands down, no other way to give it to you but raw and uncut. It's in my blood, it's who I am, it's what I been my entire life, but it took me to go to prison to discover my true identity. I'm at the top of my game right now with all flaws ironed out. This is not a game, ultimatum or none of that shit. It's an opportunity. An opportunity to go to the top and I'm asking you to go with me. Choose me Alisha, it would be the best decision you ever made in your life."

"I chose you a long time ago Threat." Alisha said now looking out the passenger's window. Her voice was low and I got the impression that she'd been expecting this. "I was raised in Orange" Alisha said, "But I wasn't born yesterday Threat. I know when I'm getting macked on. Pimps from

Houston try to holla at me all the time in the club with their lame ass rehearsed lines. But there was something different about you, that's why I let you take it this far. I never told you this but I love the way you talk. And besides, I chose you in your thrift store clothes, not this pretty Cadillac and your designer clothes. You say you have pimp in your blood, well I have hoe in mine, so I know when a Boss is in front of me. It's something that all girls know." Alisha looked at me with her exotic, hazel brown eyes, she put her hand on my leg and said, "I'm with you Threat wherever you want to take me."

Check game. Whatever is said is understood, and whatever is understood is overstood, therefore the shit don't need an explanation. I didn't say a single word; I just hit the touch screen and selected Jeremih (Feat. J. Cole) 'Planes' and listened to the hook while we continued on I-10.

Let's take a trip

Have you ever read "The World Is Yours"

On a blimp?

CHAPTER 8
WAR STRATEGIES

The Gentlemen's club, better known as Players also owned a billboard that was elevated in the sky so the motorist on I-10 could see. But the difference between this set up and Denny's is that Player's offers its service only to a particular class and status. I guarantee you won't find shit in Player's for $6.99 but maybe a two inch shot glass of tequila. Player's is a predominately white club with a handful of ballers and foreigners who most definitely proclaim the status of rich and wealthy.

Alisha and I fell behind a caravan of exotic whips. Mercedes, BMW's, Vettes, Ferrari's, Rolls Royce's and a couple of Lambos. With me driving and Alisha on the passenger's side gave the CTS all the authorization it needed to be here. All it takes is a little aggression, confidence and to top it off, two sexy muthafuckers can fill that void even if we rolled up in a Kia.

When we eventually made it to the front, we were approached by two valet parkers who looked to be in their late twenties. One black who's name tag said Chris and the other one was a red head white boy whose name tag said Brad. Both of them were wearing red vest, white button down shirts with black slacks.

Chris asked me, "Sir, would you like valet parking and a VIP booth tonight'?"

"Yeah, that's proper." I said while Alisha grabbed her back-pack and was being escorted out of the car by Brad.

When Chris drove off with the CTS, Brad asked me, "Would you like an escort to your booth while Alize goes to the dressing room or would you like to be escorted by Alize? At this point I'm thinking, Alize? It immediately shot me to the history of slavery.

See, slavery means enforced servitude, along with society's recognition that the master has ownership rights over the slave and his or her labor. The first thing the master snatches to claim ownership is the slave's name and replaces it with either his name or whatever he sees fit to cater to his establishment. If the slave can't identify with 'Self' then the slave has no other choice but to identify with the master. Still snapping back quick, I said, "No lil man, my escort here is fine."

"Okay then!" He said while handing me a yellow laminated card with the number 4 written on it. Alisha didn't waste any time snatching the card out of my hand.

She said, "Daddy you're in booth four, that's perfect because I'll be dancing on stage one, and that's right in front of your booth, already." I could tell that Alisha was excited but still containing herself so she didn't come off as desperate. She reminded me of a shorty who received company for the first time, acting hyper just out of the sense of fun. And this was fun to her no doubt. She had company and I was the guest in her house, which was more than entertainment itself.

It was an atmosphere of invitation and welcome. As soon as we walked in, we were greeted by a tall brunette who was wearing only a black G-string and the same color stilettos. She had what I would sum up to be a C Cup, a nice size ass for a white girl and a Barbie doll face. Obviously, the result of a couple of expensive face lifts, still overall I'll give her around an 8 or 8 1/2 give or take. She gave us that artificial Hollywood smile with a vibrant spark in her eyes.

Over the thumping music she said, "Really, Really Alize? So you just gonna walk in here with Mr. Casanova himself right?"

Alisha didn't say shit, she just nodded her head. Her face was blank so I automatically received the notion that maybe this is one of them messy ass hoes that Alisha was warning me about.

Channeling energy and reading body language is a top priority because it will reassure your bitch that not only do you have the ability to read in between the lines, but it will also lace her up that you and her have a silent communication with each other.

Before we pressed on, the brunette continued, "Well anyway, I think you should hurry and get dressed, Muhammad is walking around here going on a rampage."

Alisha rolled her eyes and as we were walking off she said, "I think you should worry more about you and less about me then the world would be a wonderful place."

"Whatever!"

Is all I heard in response as we made our way into the colossal club of Players. Players was popping and proper all at the same time. It was laced with white marble floors, crystal chandeliers suspended from the ceilings with light fixtures kept close, making the whole scene dim lit and comfortable. In the middle of the club is a white staircase leading to a second terrace with a glass floor. We walked pass a lounging room with several wall mounted HD flat screens with plush seating options. I noticed around eight different stage selections with stripper poles inserted at halfway point. Then we walked pass the bar and that bitch was loaded with whatever you could imagine that involved alcohol. I see a large showcase with Patron, Hennessy, Cognac, Cîroc and Grey Goose and thought; they even got something for the ballers.

There were several waitresses but the one that stood out was a smiling Filipino looking chick with long hair that hung pass her ass like a Hawaiian hula hula dancer. On top of that, there were hoes everywhere, all looking right with no bullet wounds, stab scars or tiger stripe stretch marks. Not even a cellulite in site, the whole set up looked like some shit straight outta Vegas or better yet, The Boom Boom Room.

Booth four was a high quality, luxury European style booth with maroon leather upholstery. There was even an IPad embedded inside the table for menu selections and off the muscle, I almost got heated to see one of my ideas but at the same time I understood the 'Hundredth Monkey' concept and I likewise respect the fact that great minds think alike. As soon as we were, about to sit down, another stripper approached us at the booth with rhythmic stripper dance movements, a white girl wearing a red G-string with platinum blond hair, big titties like cantaloupes with a small waist. At first glance she looked flawless but I noticed a scar underneath her chin, traveling towards her neck. It would more than likely be unnoticeable to the average eye, but see I pay attention to detail. Besides, there's nothing average about me. I'm the type of nigga that would notice a black ant crawling on a black rock on a black dark night. I also noticed that the energy was different between Alisha and this particular stripper contrary to the last one.

With a bubbly voice the white girl said, "Hey girl! So do I like have to introduce myself or are you going to introduce me?" She said with her hand extended out towards me as if she was Racheal from The Price is Right.

Alisha smiled without any sign of hostility then said, "I would introduce you right, but I think I'll let you introduce yourself, but you'll have to do it at your own risk."

"Risk?" She asked with raised eyebrows. "What's the risk?"

Alisha looked at me then back at her. She said, "This nigga right here will hypnotize your ass."

"Oh Really?"

"Yes bitch really." Alisha said. "Oh, and for future reference, don't say I didn't warn you."

Alisa and I sat down on one side of the booth while the white girl sat on the opposite side with a slow smile building up. It was no secret; you could tell from her grimacing and lip biting that she had a dying desire to understand what exactly was going on here. Didn't she understand that curiosity is what killed the cat? I felt a soft tapping at my ankle under the table. When I made eye contact with Alisha, she was nodding her head in the direction of the white girl.

Alisha contributed to her curiosity when she said, "I'm going to let you two get acquainted with each other while I go get dressed. I don't want that camel jockey saying shit to me. Oh and I'm up next so keep your eyes on stage one."

Her curiosity went off the charts when I said, "Make this performance your best performance because tonight will be the last night you'll be dancing on that stage. Tell the DJ to introduce you as your real name, you ain't no muthafucking alcohol beverage, feel me? And if anybody in this club want to contact you from this day forward, then tell them to make their business cards rain along with the dollars."

Now this is where the test comes in to see if Alisha is about that shit and is bred for this type of lifestyle. Would she give up all of this superficial wealth that don't belong to her and cross the track to see what a nigga like me is talking about? Or did I fail to convince her that I'm the real deal and not just a bunch of lip service that's currently living in a fantasy? I was more than reassured when Alisha leaned into my space and gave me a sloppy wet kiss with her soft mesmerizing mouth. But here's the hook; we both were staring at the white girl the whole time. Alisha slowly turned her head towards me then said, "It still stands Threat, and I will go wherever you want to take me."

Alisha stood up with half closed eyes, a lidded look of satisfaction. Then she winked her eye at me with a slight tilt in her head, which was directed at the white girl again. Before she left the booth she said, "Show me what Daddy is made of." If there was any doubt, at this point there should be no question that Alisha is a natural born bottom bitch. She was made for this shit without an orientation. She knows the rules and regulations without an explanation. I would like to call it a 'Hoe's Instinctive Intuition'. And, if you didn't peep the code that she telepathically communicated to me, then it went a little something like this:

> Threat, I know you're that dude, I'm here with you. Fuck this job; I was tired of this place anyway. Now get this bitch and show me what daddy can do.

When Alisha bounced I converted my attention to the white girl, I slapped on my A game and stepped up to the challenge to see if I could pull this bitch in record-breaking time.

She almost threw my concentration though because she was forming her hand like a referee then said, "Okay, time out, time out, what just happen? You mean seriously Alize won't be working here anymore?"

I decided to answer her question with a question so I said, "Everything in life has a chronological order to it. How are we going to get to point C if we haven't even left point A yet?" She scratched her temple with a blank stare and a slack expression so I knew I went over her head. See, in the game it's a cardinal rule to have the gift of gab.

As a Boss Pimp it's your call of duty to be well versed with the know how to tit for tat with a bitch toe to toe. Value your mouth piece like the weapon that it is. Would you take an unloaded 45 to a gunfight? I thought not! For this reason alone make sure your mouth is loaded at all times with a potent arsenal to open fire on a bitches brain. This is what you call the holy grail of social interaction. The ability to woo a bitch.

Off the top I knew I could cuff her with word play so I said, "Look, you expect me to answer all these elaborate questions and what not, but we haven't properly introduced ourselves yet. So this is how it's gonna go down. I'm going to give you point A. My name is Threat, Thomas Threat. I go by my last name. Don't ask me why, I just do, feel me? Now in order for us to continue on to point C with this conversation, first you have to give me point B, what's your name?"

"Star". She said. Then I quickly went into a state of Deja vu.

She has the same handle as my mom's but still didn't justify her coming at me the way she did. I rubbed my hands together as I leaned forward, I said, "I don't think you heard me correctly, I said my name is Threat not trick."

I pointed my hand in the direction of a group of white men dancing off beat with their suit jackets resting on the back of chairs. I said, "You see them over there dancing as if they're about to go into a seizure?"

She giggled then said, "Yeah".

"Yeah well those are the ones you tell that Star shit to. I'm real therefore I deserve a real name."

She smiled as if she was impressed with my aggressive demeanor and said, "My real name is Carmen."

My shoulders were shrugged with open raised palms so she caught the hint that I was waiting for more.

"Wow, you're persistent huh? Well my full name is Carmen Styles. There, is that better?"

I stared at her for a few seconds while registering the name, picturing her with the name and I couldn't call it why she would choose anything else besides her real name. So I said, "No, you should tell yourself it's better. It's a lot better than Star I'll tell you that much."

"What you don't like Star?"

"It's not that I don't like the name Star." I said. "Truth be told, I don't embrace bullshit that's unoriginal. Take a look around you. Yeah the girls in here look straight but they still have the same handles as girls in other strip clubs who don't match up to their criteria. It's like a broken record, Jasmine, Champagne, Mercedes, Star, Moet, Alize, Diamond, Coca, Moca, Loca and all that. The shit is played out! Ask yourself this. How many Stars do you think there is, not including the one's in the sky? Now ask yourself how many Carmen Styles exist? Only one! Stay original baby, Carmen Styles is the shit."

I noticed more intense visible blushing, which reminded me of the cardinal rule number one. Once you grin, you're in! The tables has turned in a matter of minutes. She is more than private, after all it's her job to invite attention, but as of right now, at this particular moment, she has no other choice but to pay attention. But still I let her make the next move because I knew what was on her mind and at the same time, it was going to work in my favor.

She asked me, "So Alize won't be working here anymore?"

"First of all, her name is Alisha; get used to it. And no she won't be working here anymore, and if you're smart you'd come with us."

"Come with you?" Carmen asked with bulging blue eyes. "Come with you where?"

"To the top, where else?" I said while I sat back and stared at her with strong eye contact. I inhaled deeply through my nose, and then exhaled through my mouth. I stood up, changed positions and sat right next to Carmen. I reached for her hand while staring into her eyes; I could smell her rogue perfume burning my nose hairs. I could see peach hairs on her titties standing up, so I knew her senses were heightened with anticipation. That's when I asked her, "Are you rich Carmen?"

"Rich? I hardly doubt it. I been living in a hotel for the past six months. Rich people don't survive off fast food and TV dinners do they?"

"Not at all," I said. "You should be eating caviar and steak on a daily basis and sipping on champagne to wash the shit down. But I'll tell you this much; the people who own this club sure do look rich to me, which brings me to my point. If you're not sharing their wealth, eating what they're eating, driving what they're driving, living where they're living, then you're just spinning your wheels on a cycle that's going nowhere. Shaking your ass is time invested, therefore at the end of the day you should have something to show for it."

I placed my arm around her shoulder then pulled her closer to me. Her bare breast, cantaloupe titties were now smothered into my chest but she seemed not to care. It was like as if she was just waiting for her knight in shining armor to come and rescue her from the pain that life had to offer. All she wanted was happiness, peace, security and a family, which I could provide all of the above. I ran my finger slowly with the direction of her scar underneath her chin. I apologized, not out of accountability but to voice the unfairness of life and the situations that caused the pain. In a mellow smooth tone, I said, "Carmen, I know you've experienced a little pain, making you feel broken inside and I apologize that you had to go through those trials. But I can guarantee you that if you come with me and Alisha you'll experience the direct opposite. You'll have everything you want and need. You'll live like, if not better than the hustlers who own this club. And to top it off, we'll be a family."

I could tell Carmen's thoughts were scattered. I could even feel her heart racing through her large titties. I read her and I knew it was a bull's eye, right on the money because she said, "Threat, you have a lot of charisma and I just love your kick ass confidence. And I'm sure you get this a lot but you are amazingly cute, oh my God. I can tell that you're not just some random person off the street because you're out of the ordinary. I mean it's like you work for the Psychic Network or something because yes I experienced something terrible. So terrible that sometimes I even feel like giving up, but I'm still holding on by a thread. All I want is to feel happy again. I want to be surrounded with family and friends. I just completely adore Alize, I mean Alisha. Sorry! We're like night and day but still we click so you know. Wow, you sure do know how to get a girl's adrenaline going don't you? My heart is beating so fast that I can't even think straight." I ran my finger slowly down her lips, making her bottom lip hang for a split second and gently kissed her forehead.

I looked directly into her baby blue eyes then and said, "Follow your heart Carmen; it's trying to tell you that with me is where you belong."

While we were staring at each other, piercing our eyes in the same direction, I felt that she suddenly gained an appreciation for the world and everything in it. Just as we were caught up in the moment, the DJ made an announcement. He made damn sure that everyone in the entire club could hear him too.

"Alright, listen up fellas and gentlemen here at the magnificent Club of Players, I have a special announcement. How many of you are familiar with the beautiful goddess that use to go by the name Alize?"

The whole club burst out in an standing ovation with roars, claps, shouts and barks. Except the brunette who was, standing close by with her arms crossed, watching with her lips pressed flat at the mention of Alisha's name. Tough titty for her hate because as soon as the crowd piped down, the DJ continued, "Notice" how I said, "'use to' go by Alize. Well fellas her real name is Alisha Farrell and tonight is the last night you will see her here at Player's because she's moving on to bigger and better things."

"Booo, Booo." Everybody set off a song to a different

tune but the DJ was flapping his hand at the crowd.

He said, "Calm down, calm down now. Alisha Farrell is making herself available, so this is what I want you to do. When she comes out on stage one, you need to throw them business cards out so she can call you for a private lap dance. She says that she gives her word that she will contact every card. Now what you think about that? So if you love Alisha Farrell, and you support Alisha Farrell, then here's your chance to give it up for; Alisha Farrell gentlemen."

The lights in the club all at once went out, making it pitch black. The only source of light at this point were the bright light coming from the screen savers from the IPads that were inserted in the tables from the VIP booths. Carmen and I were still on the same side of the booth and I still had my arm around her shoulder, making it obviously clear that I was claiming her as my prize. Besides, Alisha needs to witness that this is just a small fragment of the many wonders of what daddy can do.

Then like an instant flick of a light switch, stage one lit up with a spot light. You could see Alisha's silhouette approach the stage and the very second she entered the spot light, Salena Gomez's sexy voice pulled from the speakers.

I'm on my 14 carats
I'm 14 carat
Doing it up like Midas, mmm
Now you say I gotta touch
So good, so good
Make you never wanna leave
So don't, so don't.

Alisha was on point beyond all measures. She had on a white lace G-string, white thigh high fish net stockings and clear see through stilettos. Her curly hair was glossy with sprinkles of glitter. Her perfect eyebrows from her bottomless hazel brown eyes, all done to a perfection. Her yellow skin was glowing and her B cup titties were perky with her nipples standing tall.

While Salina Gomez was singing "Gonna wear that dress you like skin tight, do my hair up real nice."

Alisha was strutting around the pole in a flirtatious kind of way while holding it with one hand; her perfect dime piece body was extended out towards the crowd. She stopped with her backside on display. Her ass is shaped artistically and crafted like two yellow glistening soccer balls that she made jump with the single motion of her ass muscles. She slowly bent over with her hands on her hips. She looked back at the fiending crowd with her legs spread, giving them a clear shot of that gigantic camel toe print.

Oohs and aahs came from the crowd, along with dollars and business cards from all angles of the stage. Then she dropped down to a split. She bounced and popped her ass three times and came back up like a piece of cake. Alisha turned around then locked her eyes on me while Selena Gomez's sexy voice flowed through the speakers.

"Let me show you how proud I am to be yours."

Alisha was talking to me and it was the proper words to fit the occasion. She slightly tilted her head down with her eyes still locked in on me with her mouth partially open. She rolled her tongue across her lip-glossed lips. Then with her right hand, she slowly entered the front part of her white laced G-string. She erotically moved her hips in circular motions then bent her knees, making the whole movement look as if she was riding a nigga.

Damn Alisha!

My man was jumping in my pants but still I had him contained. Alisha grabbed the pole again and as soon as she got a good grip, Carmen looked at me then right back at Alisha as if she said, "Watch this!"

Alisha twirled around the pole with her legs in motion, showing extreme upper body strength. By the time she made it to the top of the pole, she made it her duty to make sure our eyes were connected.

"I just want to look good for ya, good for ya, uh huh, uh huh."

She opened her legs as wide as they could possibly go with the pole center front, right there in the middle. As soon as Selena Gomez said;

"Trust me I can take you there."

Alisha slid down the pole with her legs still spread wide open except now her neck and head was extended back. When she made it to the bottom, she crawled towards the crowd as if she was an exotic leopard and she looked as if she was possessed with sexual eroticism.

"Still look good for ya, good for ya, uh huh, uh huh."

Alisha laid on her back with both hands gripped to her titties; She closed her eyes while Selena Gomez's voice faded with the lights.

Trust me, I, trust me, I, trust me, I

When the lights came back on the crowd went crazy. They were clapping, hollering, whistling and still throwing money and business cards. Alisha stood center stage and bowed while they shouted, "Alisha Farrell, Alisha Farrell, Alisha Farrell."

Carmen walked with me towards the stage and we made our way through the crunk crowd of excited businessmen, executives and ballers. When we finally made it to the front of the stage, we held our hand out towards Alisha, suggesting for her to take our hand. Carmen and I helped Alisha down while they followed me back to the booth. I was on one side while the girls were together on the other side. Alisha was still heavily breathing but at the same time, she had an overall visage that radiates a beautiful smile. Carmen had an incredulous dazed look on her face while she had her fingers spread out in a fan against her breastbone.

"Oh my God girl that was awesome," Carmen said. "What's gotten into you?"

"Nothing yet!"

Alisha said with an animated winking eye at me. I didn't respond to the wink, I just hit the touch screen on the IPad then scrolled down until I found something decent to order.

When I made my selection, I said, "This is cause for a celebration; are you two down?"

"I'm down." Alisha said. "No need to ask."

I looked at Carmen waiting for an answer with anticipating eyes. She stood still with rigid body posture and she was tapping her fingers against the table in an effort to quickly make a decision. It was as if she went blank, making the moment awkward as hell. All you could hear was the thumping bass of Bruno Mars coming from the background. She closed her eyes, took a deep breath then finally she spoke up.

"Threat, can you please just promise me one thing?"

"Depending on what it is Carmen, Don't want to commit to something that I can't provide."

"Well can you at least promise me that we'll go somewhere with this?"

I held my hands loosely behind my back, and then I shot back with a little sarcasm.

"Can a bird fly, whistle and shit at the same time?"

They laughed and giggled. From there on we huddled up for a good ten minutes, then a smiling beautiful, black, chocolate waitress approached the booth with a bottle of Dom Perion, a stainless steel bucket of ice and three champagne glasses. I leaned in towards the waitress so I could get a good look at her nametag.

"Thank you Shanna," I said as I opened my wallet then gave her a business card. "Check it out, my name is Threat and if by chance you don't feel vindicated for your efforts, sacrifices and hard work, then give me a call."

She stared at the card with a condescending smile then wrinkled her nose like the motherfucker had shit on it or something. As she was walking off, she said, "Oh kaay!"

My ego went into over drive as I thought; bitch you been played before yes I know, but still no excuse for you to ignore, the seed that the Game God planted in hopes to sow. You can run but can't hide because sooner or later the mothafucka will grow. Still snapping back quick, I paid attention to the girls where they stood topless, standing tall wearing stilettos and G-strings. On the other hand, I'm suited and booted in all black with Armani frames on my face. I popped the Dom Perion bottle then poured a quarter of champagne in each glass. And don't you know right before we were about to make a toast, we were interrupted with a loud throat clearing sound. The club's manager, Muhammad stood before the booth while holding a purple velvet bag with the club's logo Player's written on the front.

With a high chin and flaring nostrils, the Pakistani native said with a controlled tone. "Alize, there's a rumor floating around that you intend to resign your position here at Player's." Alisha opened her mouth to say something but I thrusted my arm forward before she could utter a single word.

"I got this." I said as I walked closer to the manager. He stood at a mere 5'5 so I'm looking down at him. But he looked every bit of the least intimidated because he stood with a wide stance with protruding eyes that appeared dark and cold. He wore a black tuxedo with a solid black tie on top of a black button down shirt. He sported a sad attempt at a goatee with an extra thick mustache and a trimmed beard. His jet-black hair was slicked back with no hints of grey, which I noticed off the rip was with the assistance of a little hair color and dye. This dude had 'Compensation' written all over him. But little did he know that the nigga before him could read sense and expose bullshit in a matter of seconds. I rubbed my hands together then asked him. "What's going on Mr. Muhammad?"

His eyebrows rose at the sound of his name being mentioned by a complete stranger. He didn't say shit; he just glanced at Alisha and Carmen because he figured that's where the source of information came from. I regained his attention when I said, "I'm pretty sure you heard the DJ because he said it loud and clear. This young lady right here has a name and it's Alisha Farrell. I also heard him say loud and clear that tonight was her last night working here." I looked at the girls, I asked them, "Didn't you hear the DJ say it?" They nodded their heads yeah so I said to Muhammad, "I can't call it why everyone else in this club heard it except you?"

He tried to camouflage his anger with a weak smile and he asked me. "And you are?"

"My name is Threat?"

"Threat?" He asked with the lifting of a single eyebrow and his head was now cocked to the side. His body language clearly stated that he was demanding proof or a little evidence to support the claim that my name is actually, what I was to him right now: "A THREAT!"

I reached in my wallet then gave him a business card. However, while he was thoroughly examining the card, I said, "It's pronounced just like it's spelled... THREAT!

Peep game. I'm in the middle of a war right now. The first thing that comes in war is strategy, which is the general design behind any war, even in a military campaign. On a large scale, it involves 'Grand Strategy', but see, it can't be reduced to a set of general rules, but it always involves long-term planning.

Analyzing one's own and the enemy's strength, understanding the land, soldiers and planning moves accordingly by knowing when and where to fight. In other words, to defeat thy enemy is to know thy enemy.

I know everything about Muhammad because I studied this establishment and his staff before I came here because I figured a situation like this would jump off. Not only is Muhammad the manager, he's also the owner. This little dude is the offspring of a well-respected oil tycoon, which makes him the next dynasty. So you know Player's is nothing but Muhammad's playground. With his eyes still locked in on the card, he said, "I see that you are an artist and that is a very fine position, but according to this card, your name is Thomas not Threat."

I gave him a half grin; the kind that conveyed a secret knowledge. Then I glanced back over my shoulders at the girls, I asked them, "What's this man's name right here?"

When they both said, "Muhammad" in unison, I turned to him then said, "Ever since I walked up in this club people been referring to you as Muhammad. The brunette at the front door, even these beautiful women right now. Never, not once did you correct them, not even me when I called you Muhammad because I assume that's what you prefer; a name closer to the prophet right? But according to your shareholder documents that you have invested in this property, your name is "Hussan Muhammad!" You were born in Karachi Pakistan in 1961, so you know your name is Hussan not Muhammad; tell me what the fuck is the difference?"

We stared at each other long and hard without a single blink. I noticed beads of sweat on his forehead and if I'm not mistaken, this nigga's chin is trembling right now. His anger suddenly turned into thoughts searching for a solution to iron this situation out before it got out of control. I could hear his thoughts out loud: I have a grade, a reputation and an elite status to protect and I surely wouldn't jeopardize it due to this, this pimp. Muhammad cleared his throat then regained his composer back to reality, he said, "Let's not get beside ourselves" he said with a crackling voice. "I came to give Alize... Pardon me, Alisha her earnings for the night."

I nodded my head to Alisha, signaling for her to get the bag. When she walked over to get the bag, Muhammad asked her, "So are you sure about this?" Alisha poked her tongue lightly into her cheek and inhaled a long breath. "Uh, duh! What do you think this is a practical joke or something? Hell yeah I'm sure!" He switched his attention to a different direction because he's already accepted the cold hard fact that he just lost the best girl in the entire club.

"Star, does this stand with you as well? Surely you have enough snap not to fall for this nonsense don't you?" She leaned in forward with her hands on the table and with a slow smile building up, she said, "Yeah, I guess you are being punk'd because my name is Carmen; little man."

Muhammad walked off with his hands in the air, which was his peaceful way of surrendering. We cracked up laughing so hard that my eyes were tearing up, Carmen's face was red and Alisha was shaking her head emphatically. Alisha said through her laughs, "I ain't had a laugh like that since my brother stuck a pencil in the wall socket. He said that was how they lit cigarettes in the pen. His dumb ass electrocuted himself and spent the whole day with a stupid ass grin on his face."

"That's good shit." I said with a chuckle. "Now get yourselves together because we got something important to take care of."

They followed my lead as we all picked up our quarter full champagne glasses and held them at shoulder length. At this particular moment, I received a satisfaction with the world at large and felt connected to the gods who created this lifestyle. I slowly closed my eyes to savor this experience. With open body posture, I released an appreciative sigh and opened my eyes, and in a mellow tone I said. "We are now initiating a body of associates, all on the same page of money seeking endeavors. In this event, you chose me to guide and protect you as we climb the ladder to success. Anything less than the top is unacceptable. I am your pimp and you are my bitch, nothing more, nothing less. You will stay in pocket, you will keep your emotions in check and I shall do the same. Nothing, no one or anything imaginable will derail this money train. This is a toast to greatness."

We all put our glasses together making the toast. Then I said, "This is a drink to success."

We took one sip from our glass then bounced. We left the Dom, ice and three glasses on the VIP booth's table. I paid the bill up front while the girls got dressed. I also left the waitress a nice tip. Every penny spent was toward some type of investment one way or another. Before we left, I wrote a note on the back of the receipt and asked the clerk to make sure Muhammad received it. He will read it as it says:

You will hear from me soon. I know what you want! In

the meantime, in between time... Thanks for the girls. Threat.

CHAPTER 9
PSYCHOLOGICAL BAGGAGE

A pimp cannot pimp without a hoe. Charisma is a mystical or magical gift most pimps have, the ability to transform even regular 9 to 5 working bitches into devoted and enthusiastic prostitutes. There's even social scientist investigating the behavior of pimps to understand what gives a pimp charisma. But social psychologist are more interested in the emotional responses that hoes have towards a pimp's behavior.

The emotional responses that a pimp produce in any hoe is front page shit because a major part of the game is motivating your hoes to work toward a particular goal. For example, an entrepreneur jumping off a startup company might motivate employees to work as hard as they can for long crazy hours with little to no pay with only a small shot at success. A completely rational mothafucka would bounce somewhere else.

Instead, many stay because of how the project and the CEO made them feel, especially about themselves. If you got what it takes to make a hoe feel good about herself in the event of selling pussy then you've just tapped into the initiation process it takes in developing charisma. My pimp tight advice is to start with the name. You might think, what's in a name? The power of a name is an example of a more general process society like to call labeling. Labels categorize an individual as belonging to a certain role or class of people. It's like this; if you continuously label shorty as bad, then guess what's gonna go down? That shorty is going to identify as being bad so you can expect him to continue doing bad shit. But if you tell that same so-called bad shorty that he's doing excellent and that he's an intelligent kid, then you will convince him that he's the kid you would like him to be. We use labels to socially construct reality. With the right techniques, you can construct a better reality.

The power of labels to create reality can be seen clear as daylight in the importance we attach to names. When you hear the names Champagne, Moet, Alize, Star, Candy, Diamond, Ginger et cetera; what's the first thing that pops up in your mind? Stripper bitch right? The reality of them taking off their clothes for money will never change. But just like the bad kid, you give them a first rate label; you know, something like their real name then they will feel good about themselves, thus becoming the best strippers or prostitutes that you could ever imagine. Why? Because they hear their real names being promoted, something like a celebrity. In today's world, almost every bitch wants to either be or feel like a damn celebrity.

So now, here I am a halfbreed nigga fresh out the pen

with two celebrities, Alisha Farrell and Carmen Styles. Carmen's hotel room at the La Quinta Inn is around 20 minutes away from the club so we had enough time to build. My intentions were to get down and gritty so I could peep her mental structure to find out what besides my charisma motivated her to embrace my pimping.

I started a thorough evaluation by first asking where her car was. She said that she pays people to drive her here and there, considering she hasn't driven a vehicle in over eight years, Ever since the accident!

The state of Texas puts out an official booklet each year of rules of the road, but there's no textbook that teaches the art of driving itself. So people like Carmen don't have the slightest clue of what your 'Blind Spot' means or the importance of observation when actually behind the wheel.

Eight years, three months and one week ago to be exact, she was sideswiped by a drunk driver who ran a red light coming from the intersection. She survived the crash but unfortunately her four year old son who's seatbelt wasn't properly fastened didn't make it. Since then she's been repeatedly evaluating herself by going over and over in her mind what actually went down. Too much self-focus can lead anybody to analyze and reanalyze the tape but fail to realize that they can't rewind time. Which is why she went into that self-blame state, thinking it's going to help her recover but it only lead her into a funk of depression. She's also developed a strong phobia because she never touched a steering wheel again since the day of the accident.

So here, I come into the picture, a nigga who knows the symptoms of depression. The common signs are sadness, loss of interest and pleasures in life's activities, fatigue, and feeling like you ain't shit and thoughts of suicide. Depressed people are attracted to aggression and possess the natural tendency to roll with the 'Bad Boy' who will place them in either a negative environment or situation. I reignited life back into Carmen's consciousness with excitement, living on the edge, which now all of a sudden she's concerned about going somewhere with this. In this case. I'm not only her knight in shining armor but I'm also her doctor. The one, who she confides in, honors with respect and trust, even if I tell her that I would have to remove one of her kidneys. No questions asked except how long would the procedure take?

As I lay here on Carmen's bed with my hands behind my head, I look at her hotel room and notice scattered clothes everywhere, fast food bags with leftover food on the table. But on the dresser next to the TV is a 5x9 framed picture of her son Kobey. He's a good-looking kid, blond like his moms with the same blue eyes and a matching vibrant smile. He resembled Carmen in a remarkable way, which made me ask myself, where the fuck was the daddy? She never mentioned him so I'm guessing he was a sperm donor or just a distant memory that she'd rather forget.

Like Mack once said, today is the first day of the rest of her life. At 29 years old, this is a new beginning, a fresh start where she can iron out her emotional dejections and link up with a team that's encircled by greatness, with a goal and an extravagant lifestyle. She has talent and enormous potential but it takes a nigga like myself to show her what she's capable of doing.

As of right now, I'm reading her energy and I can't help but notice that she's in a playful mood. She has big movements with leaps across the small hotel room with happy bursts of screaming, laughing and giggling with Alisha. She has a bright outlook of the situation and a burning desire to spread joy and make damn sure we feel the same. Now that's what you call southern hospitality. But I sensed something else in the air, I mean since she shot it out there.

"So who's gonna take a shower first?"

Before anyone could speak up, she said, "Okay, guess I will."

Then Alisha rushed her with a pillow. She struck Carmen in the dome with one single shot, and then shouted, "Not without me."

This crunk up a full fledge pillow fight. They attacked each other with the pillows, which eventually lead to the ground. They wrestled like two WWE girls but the only difference between these two girls is that they had uncontrollable laughs. Carmen was no match for Alisha though, because Alisha now had her pinned to the ground with tickles as Carmen screamed for mercy. But Alisha wasn't rising up without a price.

"Who's your daddy bitch? Who's your daddy? Huh, huh?"

Carmen shouted at the top of her lungs so the lady at the front desk could hear. "Threat's my daddy, Threat, Threat, Threat, Threat! That's who bitch!"

Alisha's eyes widened with raised eyebrows then glanced at me as if looking for approval. I raised my hands up, allowing the silence to do the talking. Then Alisha went right back in with more tickling.

While watching them bullshit around I notice the sheer pleasure of them playing around and being here at this particular moment in time. Not having one single worry or regret for choosing me as their daddy. One who watches over his shorties while playing around in complete obliviousness to the dangers that life had to offer. Yet still they trust me like a shorty would trust their old man to catch them while jumping off a moving swing. Yeah, I got you!

They both ran to the shower, leaving their clothes with the other dirty clothes that were already on the floor. This habit is gonna have to stop because my OCD won't allow this shit to be habitable. But dig, there's a perfect time and place for everything. Right here, right now is no place or time to be sweating small shit, so by all means I got to let it ride. But what I won't let ride is the fact that I got two beautiful women in the shower together right now. What, you think I ain't gonna put it down? I'm fresh on the blacktop with two hoes strong so my feet is shallow deep in the game after twelve long years, it's time to get my dick wet by two anticipating dames.

I took my clothes off and hung them up on a hanger in the closet because I knew I wouldn't need them again until the morning. I put my glasses inside the pocket of my suit jacket and got the package of Trojans that I knocked off at the Valero. I threw them on the bed for easy access then made my way to the bathroom.

As soon as I quietly opened the door, the steam coming from the shower momentarily had me blind to the point where I couldn't see shit in front of me. But, I clearly heard Alisha and Carmen giggling behind the shower door. I recognized Carmen's voice.

"What do you think he's doing?"

"Girl trust, he knows what time it is." Alisha said.

I took my boxers off then slid the shower door open. That's when all conversations and giggling came to a halt. All you could hear at this point was the water discharging from the showerhead. They both froze with bulging eyes and Carmen's grip to Alisha's arm tightened with increased swallowing.

Then finally, Alisha spoke up "I told you. What I tell you. Girl we struck gold."

"O.M.G." Carmen said with her eyes locked in on my dick.

I entered the shower and they both, without procrastinating started lathering up my body with bodywash. The warm water from the showerhead slowly trickled down my back while Carmen was rubbing the soap foam to my chest and abs. With fascination in her eyes, she said, "He looks like an action figure."

Alisha didn't bullshit around; she stroked my dick with a soft caressing gesture. She applied more bodywash to it then said, "Look, it even gets bigger."

While they were focused in on me, I was examining their perfect physical structure and thought to myself; should I call this luck, skill, fate or all the above? Carmen's large titties with the Daytona beach bikini tan line to Alisha's apple bottom ass, slim waistline and her Queen Nefertiti golden skin. I never would have guessed that you could find this type of breed in a small country town in Texas. But I guess even Marilyn Monroe was just another country bitch that came from the back woods of a farm.

My dick was getting harder by the second after we dried off and I lead their buck-naked bodies to the bed. I turned Alisha around on all fours while she had her face in between Carmen's legs. I knew the night was about to get X-rated so I slapped a condom on just in case my lil man decided to slide in without a helmet. I watched Alisha tease Carmen's pussy with her tongue and for a split second, I was trying to decide if I wanted to either watch this freak show or participate in it. It didn't take long to choose the later because when I felt the moisture between Alisha's legs from the back, I knew she had an itch that needed to be taken care of and I most definitely knew just the right trick. Alisha's back was precisely arched when I made my entrance. I found myself shaking my head because at this point the voices were coming in strong. "Threat, Threat, Threat." However, I be damn if I was going to allow a mediocre hallucination to fuck up a wet dream. With the exception of what I was hearing inside my own dome, I still gained my rhythm. I watched my dick disappear and reappear in and out of her now soaking wet pussy. She let off a series of soft moans while she threw that ass back at me. "Mm, mmm, yeah daddy just like that."

My dick was now harder than a block of ice, so I fucked her full blast. With each hard stroke, Alisha's ass cheeks bounced up and down and her screams were now louder than the ones I was hearing inside my dome.

"Oh Threat, yes, yes, yes, yes daddy, yes. Just like that. Mmm, fuck yes!"

Carmen pulled up from underneath Alisha's face then came up next to me. We kissed while I still fucked Alisha one hundred miles per hour. I fingered Carmen's throbbing wet pussy and sucked her growing nipples while my hips were in motion. Alisha's screams suddenly went silent so I knew she was reaching her climax. I dicked Alisha down so hard that the last stroke sent her flying down to her stomach. She lay stretched out on the bed while Carmen whispered in my ear. "I want you to fuck me like that."

I lay on my back and my dick was standing up like a flagpole. Alisha's juices were all over the condom and glistening all in my pubic hairs, but Carmen didn't seem to give a fuck because she saddled up and took a pony ride. Her back was faced me while she leaned back and balanced herself on one arm. Initially she rode my dick in circular motions, and then her body switched up to something a little more exotic and barbaric because she started popping that pussy up and down my dick as if she was twerking to the rhythm of a Two live Crew anthem. "Don't stop, get it, get it. Don't stop, get it, get it." I had to keep in mind that this bitch was a stripper so she's also a class act when it comes to fucking.

When I felt Alisha's soft mouth on my balls while I was fucking Carmen, I almost exploded, but I don't have an erectile dysfunction so I turned up the volume. I grabbed Carmen's hair from the back of her head, I pulled her closer to me, then shot nothing but hard pipe directly up her stomach while I was trying to rip apart her insides. I could tell that Carmen and Alisha were kinky, borderline abusive freaks because they both enjoyed the pain.

After Carmen shouted out at the top of her lungs, "I'm cumming, I'm cumming, oh, oh, oh, oh my God I'm cumming." Alisha timed it smack dab on the money because right before I was about to skeet, she snatched my dick out of Carmen's pussy, tore the condom off my dick and stole the prize. Alisha swallowed every last drop while I laid paralyzed because it felt as if my soul was leaving my body. I still heard my name being called inside my head but I didn't sweat it. I just closed my eyes and smiled. I was beginning to become accustomed to the fact that all three of us came with psychological baggage.

CHAPTER 10
GOD WILL PROVIDE

I'm usually the first one to wake up before anyone else around me. But, this morning I was awaken by two beautiful goddesses.

One on my left and the other on my right, giving me a nice dome polish that sent shivers down my spine. All I could see was a dark curly head and a platinum blond enclosed around my dick as if it were their morning breakfast. Alisha's mouth is extremely soft, going well beyond any ordinary mouth that I ever experienced. In addition, Carmen has professional skills because she can take all twelve inches down her throat without the slightest indication of gagging. I can most definitely get use to starting my mornings off like this.

We took showers and while we were just about done getting dressed, there was a knock at the door. I opened the door to see a short Hispanic lady maybe in her late 40's with a tight fitting maid's uniform on, with cleavage on display from three open buttons on her blouse. In a heavy accent, she asked me.

"Ju no like room service ahora?"

I noticed on her nametag it said Urma so I said to her in Spanish, "Yes Urma, this place needs a good cleaning and if you do a good job, I might need you to come work for me."

She gave me a silent look then asked me, "Doing what?"

Still in Spanish, I said, "The same thing you do here, but only fulltime." I gave her a business card then said, "Call me when you make up your mind."

I stepped out of the hotel and whistled for the girls to do the same so Urma could get straight to work. They wasn't too pleased by the unexpected rush, especially Carmen because she never accepts room service. A matter fact, she goes out of her way to make sure she makes a special note to the front desk informing them just that, NO room service for room #216! But see, one thing they don't need to get use to is their natural course of things because a lot of shit is about to change around here.

When they eventually came out, I noticed that Alisha wasn't taking any chances though because she was carrying the velvet moneybag that she earned from Player's last night. When we got to the lac, I popped the trunk and she already knew what time it was. She tossed the moneybag in the trunk then made her way to the passenger's seat. Carmen sat in the back then we pressed on with our day of errands.

First thing's first; we stopped at Starbucks and got two lattes for the girls and an orange juice for me. We went to IHOP and chowed down on steak and eggs with asparagus on the side. You should have seen all the stares I received. I left my suit jacket in the lac so I wouldn't stand out, but still looking fly as fuck so people are gonna look regardless, it's almost inevitable. But damn, they didn't even play it off, hide it or be discreet about the shit. They just gawked a nigga down as if I just stepped straight up off the mothership or something.

I never completely understood why people stared at muthafucker's they didn't know. Maybe it was motivated by envy and jealousy, or it could be that they were determined to place me in a negative category so they could have more shit to gossip about on their way home. Miserable people feed off negative energy, without it they wouldn't have shit else to do. Either way, it's all live because while they kept me under surveillance, I felt fortunate that I could oblige them with some sexy ass entertainment, feel me?

We stopped at my sister's crib where I loaded the trunk with the rest of my clothes and electronics. Maya must have been in a rush this morning because the front door and gate was unlocked. She knows I have a key, but I didn't give it much thought because my mind was now focused on the damn bars that still exist on the door and windows. I felt like going to the lac, get the crowbar from the trunk and just start ripping that shit off right here right now. But I kept my cool and wrote Maya a note instead:

> What's good sis? I dropped by to get my things. I don't know if you realize it or not but the front door was unlocked. Don't get caught slipping to the point where you get too comfortable not to secure up. And why are these bars still on the house? It's not a game Maya, do something about it or else I will.

Oh, before I forgot, I may need you in the near
future. I will shoot you an email with the details.
Love ya, and stay on point.

Threat.

We swung by Alisha's house to pick up her clothes and
car. She asked me if I wanted to come in, which I was
hesitant at first but then I thought fuck it, we'll just go in
and bounce right back out. Carmen was insistent on helping
so she came in behind us. As soon as we stepped in: there
her mom's was by the window. She was humming an old
church song. "Lord you brought me from a long ways off."
She was staring out the window and it seemed as if she was
kicking around something in her mind and it was weighing
heavy on her.

I didn't even think she knew we were standing there in
the living room until she said, "Your brother is out there in
dem streets, lord knows what he's getting himself into."

"What you mean momma, that ain't nothing new?"
Alisha asked in a sarcastic tone.

Her mom's, Mrs. Brusourd now directed her attention
towards us for the first time. You could tell she was a
showstopper, straight heart breaker back in her day. Here
today she was a pleasant looking lady, maybe in her early
50's. There were a total of six gray hairs sticking up at odd
angles throughout her long shoulder length hair. Her
complexion is light skin and she resembled the late Corretta
Scott, King. Even her figure, which explained Alisha's
exotic features. Mrs. Brusourd said, "He cut his monitor off
this time and dem folks been by here twice looking for him.

I don't know how much more of this foolishness I can take. I try to tend to that boy the best I know but he can't seem to keep from trouble."

"He's probably chasing after that girl."

"Who, Jessica? Mrs. Brusourd said. "She brung her little hot tail over here last night looking for him. Don't nobody know where that boy at. Ray is driving around the Navy Edition and dem Oat Apartments right now to see if he can find him before dem folks do."

"Then what momma? What you gonna do when you find him?" Alisha asked Mrs. Brusourd with her shoulders shrugged and palms held upward.

"Prayer, we gon pray for that boy and cast that demon out and reclaim my baby. Don't you believe in prayer anymore Alisha?"

"Prayer?" Alisha said. "How bout a damn belt?"

"Don't you go talking like that in this house. What's wrong with you little girl, you losing your sense of mind or something?"

Alisha smacked her lips and rolled her eyes with one hand above her head, and said, "Look, I don't have time for this. Maybe how you be talking to me is how you should be talking to your fugitive son."

Alisha took off towards her room leaving us with Mrs. Brusourd. She looked at us, I'm guessing to see what we thought about the situation at hand. I took a quick glance at Mrs. Brusourd then at Carmen. Carmen was combing her hair with her fingers and she had her eyes locked in on her cell phone as if now, all of a sudden she was preoccupied with her emails. So now, it was me alone to deal with this family drama. Mrs. Brusourd had her eyes locked in on me with frowning eyebrows. I felt her eyes burning into me.

She was studying me and right then at that moment I felt like she could see through my soul. She could read my mind, no doubt, so I kept my thoughts simple as she asked me.

"And who are you?"

I cleared my throat, "Um, yes ma'am, excuse my manners but my name is Threa... Thomas."

Telling her my name was Threat would have took another 20 to 30 minutes explaining why I preferred to be called something that indicated trouble. She crossed her legs then placed her hand on her knees, then shot back.

"Who are you to Alisha?"

Who am I to Alisha? How in the hell am I supposed to answer that shit? What does she expect me to say? Let's see; well it's like this Mrs. Brusourd, but um, I'm her pimp and I intend to take your daughter away from this drama scene so we can get it on with the money, show her shit that she never seen before. You know, the basic shit that sums up a player ass lifestyle?

I knew that although Mrs. Brusourd was a God fearing woman, currently saved and living under God's law, but she still knew the game. I had to tell the truth and be a little crude by playing with her intelligence and going over her head all at the same time.

Still snapping back quickly, I said, "I'm her manager ma'am. Last night we walked out of that club, quit and if it's up to me we won't be looking back. The three of us put our heads together and came up with a sufficient business plan to where we can build an income from online marketing in data communications. It's a competitive field but with long hours and dedicated work we'll succeed. Alisha is getting familiar with new software, something like on the job training. But she catches on fast so it will all work out fine."

Mrs. Brusourd gave a hard sigh with an exaggerated upward glance at the ceiling, then said, "Oh my good lord, everybody these days running to that computer stuff, thinking it has all the answers to everything. I see people getting themselves into debates, the first thing they say is "let me Google it" or whatever that nonsense is called."

She reached for her bible that was resting on the coffee table. She picked it up then said, "This right here baby has all the answers you need. You get yourself in the word and the lord will provide. It says in Matthew 6:26, Behold, the fowls of the air, for they sow not, neither do they reap, nor gather into barns, yet your heavenly father feeds them. Are you not much better than they? Jehovah Jireh! The good lord will provide son."

Alisha came back with several bags of luggage and she was running back and forth for more. Carmen seen this as a grand opportunity to fall back so she picked up the bags that was on the floor and ran them to Alisha's car. I was still standing there while glancing around as if looking for answers, or better yet, an exit. Alisha was a life saver because she bailed me out when she came back with the last bags.

"Well momma, I'll keep in touch, I hope everything works out and that boy don't drive you crazy. But I'm moving on with my life so I can finally be out yall's hair."

Mrs. Brusourd stood up from the couch, walked over to Alisha and placed both of her hands to Alisha's cheeks. With an affectionate mother's touch, she politely moved Alisha's cruly hair from her face then looked directly into her hazel brown eyes with a smile that had a genuine build and it lit up her entire face. In a caring tone she said, "I'm always gonna be here for you baby. But the main thing you need to understand is that the good Lord is with you at all times. Reach out to him and he will guide your way. He did it for me, He can do it for you too."

Alisha hugged her mom's with a solid tight embrace, while Mrs. Brusourd lightly rubbed her back. The parting hug lasted longer than normal but it wasn't unusual for this moment. This was an intense, personal attachment that was sheltered somewhere deep within. I knew not to get in between a mother and her child in a situation like this so I picked up the rest of the bags and bounced as quietly as I could.

CHAPTER 11
HISTORY LESSON

Carmen rode shotgun with me while Alisha followed the lac from behind. I found myself constantly looking through my rearview mirror to see if I could make eye contact with Alisha. I suddenly developed a strong need to know exactly what she was thinking right now. Through the mirror her expression appeared pensive and I noticed she was running her hand through her curly hair. I'm just hoping that her mom's words didn't penetrate her mental because the last thing I need right now is for my bottom bitch to jump ship for a religious trip.

I like to consider myself a modern, educated nigga who's not easily influenced by hocus pocuses or organized religions.

Organized religions to me is just another institution who loses control when people like myself think critically and challenge authority, which is why they want you to have a whole lot of faith instead of a whole lot of intellect. Don't get it twisted, faith is a virtue in some situations, but not if it's used to stop critical thinking and the desire to question and learn. A lot of legitimate information has been shelved because it would make muthafuckers think and question too much.

But check it out, by the time we made it back to the room it was a quarter pass two o'clock. When Carmen opened the door we were introduced with the element of surprise. Urma did her magic and like abracadabra, the hotel room was clean from the floor up, relaxed and on point. The comforter on the bed was free of stains and professionally tucked in between both mattresses. The pillows were fluffy with icy white linen and all the clothes were washed and neatly folded and placed inside the dresser drawers. In the bathroom there were clean folded towels, hand sanitizer and seashell molded soap on the countertop, which gave the whole bathroom a floral sent.

Our environments at the highest energetic level should be spotless and clean which will allow it to define who we are. When surrounded with a clean environment, we are attracted for a more proper and deeper meaning than meets the eye. The intelligence of a clean living space has the magic and the power to harmonize with our inner beings. I can now breath, I can now think, therefore we can now take care of business.

I sat Carmen down in front of the laptop and pressed for her to find a house for sale. After a week of searching high and low for a particular house in a specific location, a realtor finally called us from The National Association of Real Estate Boards with a perfect match. A five bedroom, colonial style, two story home located in a private community six miles north of Orange called Little Cypress. The home is solid brick with beautiful landscaping and still life statues with tasteful nudes. The house is secluded with no nosy ass neighbors and to top it off, it also comes with a private long street that extends from the main street and leads to the circle driveway.

Inside it features a versatile floor plan with ornate moldings, arched walkways and columns. The formal living room has a two story sky high ceiling, maybe eighteen feet with windows ten feet from the floor, a fireplace, a walk in wet bar and millwork.

There's polished wood flooring, a cedar wood staircase leading to the master bedroom with a gigantic walk in closet that has enough space to fit my clothes, Carmen's and believe it or not but Alisha's shit too. The bedroom also has a balcony overlooking the swimming pool, a master bathroom with a glass tiled shower and fly ceiling fans.

The house was financed through my bank, all beneficiary due to art, book sales and A1 credit. It still cost a pretty penny because after paying a mortgage down payment, property taxes, home owner's insurance and mortgage clauses, I was damn near broke. All in all, the house was almost final except there was one thing missing. It was bucknaked! Although my funds were almost on E, I still had a backup plan to furnish the house. Yup, yup, the almighty plastic!

I contacted the best interior decorator I knew and Maya was more than elated to take up the project. But knowing my sister the way I knew my sister, I shouldn't have been surprised to find out that it came with a dilemma. After giving her all my credit cards I was kicked out of my own damn house. The girls and I stayed at the Regency Inn in orange until she was finished. One week and two days later, I finally received an overdue text: THE HOUSE IS READY COME CHECK IT OUT!

Knowing Maya you'll also know that she had to give us a formal orientation. We used the Camaro so when we pulled up in the circle driveway behind the lac and Maya's SUV, she was waiting for us outside and I could tell she was on the edge because she was hiding a smile behind her hand and lightly bouncing on her toes. My sister might have a serious bipolar disorder because she can switch up from silly to square business in a matter of seconds; I'm talking about a complete 180. Before she opened the door she quoted Erykah Badu, "Now keep in mind that I'm an artist and I'm sensitive about my shit."

The girls giggled but I simply checked my watch then checked my fingernails for dirt, then brushed the lint away from my shirt. I was deliberately trying to look impatient so Maya could get on with it. She caught on to the hint because as she was opening the door, she said, "Okay, Mr. ants in his pants, as you can see here in the foyer I kept it simple with an Italian style Chippendale stand to prepare you for what comes next. Walking in makes you feel like you've just entered an exclusive art gallery doesn't it?"

She opened her arm towards the living room, suggesting for us to walk in before her and the girls gasped at the first sight of the scene. Behind us Maya said, "The living room opens to the library which reveals Threat's love of art and books, giving it a perfect balance between modern and transitional, blending style of sophistication and ease."

Scoping out the house, I suddenly felt like I was on an episode of Horne Makeover. Maya tricked out the entire house as fly as you can imagine. The first thing that you notice is my art, all framed and matted at eye level view in black and white prints. All the books that I read over the years are on display on a chromed metal based library with a stainless steel ladder. There's Italian furniture in the formal living room with a custom rug that highlights a crescent moon Ralph Pucci sofa. But a large chandelier masterfully hanging from the high ceiling dominates the space. Thin fabricated drapes, allowing light to shine through the ten foot windows was a genius idea from Maya because you can never go wrong with natural light.

Black and white pimp legend photography with red frames are aligned with the staircase. This leads the way to the master bedroom which was laced with extra wide night tables, an elongated headboard and smoked glass mirrors on each side of the bed, giving the room a larger look and adding, as Maya said, "A dramatic flair." A Calvin Klein chaise rest in front of the only, TV in the house, a 60inch wall framed HD TV. Maya knows me like a book because if I'm up then a damn television is the last thing on my mind unless I'm paying attention to the bullshit news channels.

The kitchen was basically on point from the get go but Maya put her artistic touch to it with state of the art kitchen appliances and a rack hovering over the island with stainless steel pot and pans hanging from it. In the breakfast area there's Fitzgerald chairs and a white kitchen table.

The guest rooms are simply designed with custom wallpaper. One room Maya put a world map with the words 'Worldwide' written above it. Ottoman chairs, computer desk and full size beds are in each guest room. But my favorite space of the entire house is a room that she converted into a computer room. Three Oakwood desk overwhelm the room with a desk top computer, a lap top, tablets, file cabinets and three leather rolling desk chairs. On the wall is a large portrait of my old man Double T and my mom's Star. He's reclining in an oversized thrown style chair with my mom's on his right side and several other hoes are laying on the floor in position directly before his feet. It was my first time seeing the picture as Maya explained its history.

"This picture I thought you'd like because it was taking at the height of dad's prosperity. He gained a reputation for the greatest ideas and his success in Chicago and what he did in surrounding states earned him the title, 'King of The Mid West.' Mom was only 19 years old at the time of this picture but she was his main girl."

Carmen raised her hand as if she was in elementary school and we were now on a field trip at a museum listening to Maya gives a lecture on Alexander The Great. Maya giggled then walked over to Carmen, giving her a playful pinch to her arm and in response she gave Carmen a little witty commentary.

"I know I'm important and all, but girl you don't have to raise your hand. Remember, I'm a guest in your house."

"Yeah I know." Carmen said. "But your presentation and creativity is so cool, it was like my first reaction. But wow, your parents are beautiful; I can see where you two get your good looks."

Carmen giggled, as she approached the picture she touched my mom's blond hair making it seem like she could feel the physical texture, like she could actually run her fingers through the numerous fine filaments growing from her skin. She appeared fascinated as if she made some type of connection, a special bond of common interest. Still locked in on the picture, Carmen said, "Your mom looks like a super model, I mean literally like she has all the characteristics; tall, flawless skin, radiant smile, pearly whites and an awesome body."

She slowly turned around from the picture then asked Maya.

"What's her name?"

Before Maya answered with Star, I quickly shot in a short stop with the proper response, including a little history.

"Her name is Samantha Richardson." I said. "And she's from Aurea, Illinois. She was born in 1960 to a very filthy rich couple, Patrick and Geraldine Richardson. Some foul shit was going down in that household so at the age of 16 she ran away and landed in my dad's hands in Chicago. He trained and preserved her until she was 18. And what you mean look like a super model? Everything about her is super. She even turned down a modeling gig at the Playboy Mansion to rock with my dad. Everything about her is super to the point that everybody wanted my mom's. Even her own dad!"

Maya and Alisha looked at me, both with raised

eyebrows but Carmen turned towards the picture again and stared at it in silence. She looked like she was giving her heartfelt apologies, as if she had the desire to fix the past. I began tossing up thoughts inside my dome and I had to ask myself if Carmen and my moms shared more in common than I realized. Where and who does Carmen come from? What's her story? Was she molested growing up by a sick pedophile father who thought he could have any and everything, including his own child just because he had loot?

Like I said, there's a time and place for everything and the time is not now but in due time I will unravel her past like a historian.

CHAPTER 12
KNOW YOUR WORTH

Saturday morning we broke the house in proper. You know, in a player kinda way. Best believe that because we had sex everywhere. The kitchen, on the stairs, in the living room, on the bathroom countertop and we even took advantage of having no neighbors by fucking in the pool. After three rounds of fucking, I swam laps while Carmen and Alisha chased each other around the pool bucknaked with their titties and hair swinging in opposite directions. They eventually settled down and I noticed that they were applying heavy coats of suntan lotion on each other while they laid on beach towels with the sun beaming down on their naked bodies.

A little pass two o'clock Alisha showed off her Mexican side by whipping up beef enchiladas, burritos and black beans. We had chips and salsa on the side and a bowl of guacamole that she made from scratch. Alisha said she learnt the recipe from her mom's. My guess is that Mrs. Brusourd use to cook the shit for her Mexican clientele back in New Mexico as bait. Food & Sex! What a bad combination. It will have the whole barrio coming back for more.

Before nightfall we linked up in the computer room. We were all casually dressed in shorts and T-shirts but our mental was formally suited and booted for work. Getting to the money at this point was top priority because I basically cashed out on the house and my credit is now pass it's limit. I was eye popping surprised to find out that both girls have bank accounts and they were stacked up with a little over eight stacks between the both of them. Let me get that up off you. Like Big Daddy Kane once said: Romance without finance is a goddamn nuisance.

But all in all, they knew I wasn't strong arming them. They trusted the fact that I'm a go getta and that every penny invested will come back three folds. Besides, after copping this house they been spinning is wild circles, telling jokes and cracking up every five minutes. They are more than happy, they are content and they are most definitely made believers beyond any shadow of doubt, that they are now, undoubtedly fucking with a real nigga.

After Carmen logged off from their bank statements, I asked Alisha.

"Where's the money bag from Player's?"

She didn't say shit, she just went to the closet and reached up on her tiptoes for the bag. She slid the bag on the desk then confidently said, "It's right here."

"Why was it in the closet?" I asked without the slightest clue.

"Because after your sister hooked this room up as a

computer room, I put it in here because I figured you'd want to use it for business reasons."

I didn't come back with a response. I just nodded my head in agreement and glanced at the ceiling while I silently said in my mind: Thank you Game God for sending me a champion, first class, bottom bitch. I was convinced that everything is going to go straight laced with the plan. Carmen was patiently sitting in the computer chair in front of the desktop waiting for instructions and Alisha was sitting on the other desk by the laptop.

I looked at both of them saying, "Alright listen up, first thing's first. Alisha, what I want you to do is count the money but first count all the business cards. Carmen, I need you to set up an email account under the user name 'Threat To The World Entertainment'. Once Alisha is done counting the cards, I want you to save the card names to the contacts. Use Gmail for the email account and send out a massive email invitation with an ecard to every contact. You with me?"

"Yeah, just hold on a sec." Carmen said. Normally I'd be plexed up behind a bitch requesting, or even suggesting for me to hold on, but I seen that she was desperately on the hunt for a pen and paper so I compromised. I opened the desk drawer that was closest to the floor then came out with a writing tablet and an extra fine pen with the words 'CHEVROLET' written on it. I asked her, "Is this what you're looking for?"

She didn't say yeah, thank you or none of that shit. She just positioned the pen to the tablet and ready to write, she asked me, "So use the user name 'Threat To The World

Entertainment', Gmail for the account and ecard for the invites?"

"No doubt," I said. "And, I want you to phrase the invitations in your own words. Give the information in detail: Private party at discrete upscale location one week from now, next Saturday starting at 8:00 PM until. Formal attire event includes alcohol, food, pool side entertainment, indoor and outdoor sex of any girl of your liking. Party features Alisha Farrell and Carmen Styles, plus many other exotic playmates to choose from.

I gave Carmen a piece of paper with numbers written on it then continued.

"Send this account number to each invite and tell them once a thousand dollars is deposited into the account, you will send a membership card and location."

Alisha cleared her throat, as she figured was the most courteous way to interrupt without coming off as ignorant. I could tell she was ready to get on with it because she was sitting next to the laptop clicking her fingernails against the desk and there was a little tension in her face. She had everything organized in a systematical order. The money was stacked in individual stacks according to each bill. Stacks of ones, fives, tens, twenties, fifties and hundreds. The business cards were neatly stacked in what it appeared to be rows of twenty per stack. I gave her a 'What's Up?' nod, giving her the green light to take the floor. Off the top, she said, "Okay, there's some weird stuff going on in this bag but first you'll be proud of your girl to know that there's over two thousand dollars."

"Two thousand dollars?" Carmen asked with her head

jerked back.

"Mmmhmm." Alisha said. "Two thousand, three hundred and forty-two dollars."

Carmen's hands dropped to her side as she said. "That has to be like some kind of record or something I remember Safari made over twelve hundred dollars in one night and everyone went bazerk. The average is like five or six hundred dollars and that's before Muhammad dips his greasy hands in the money bag."

"Are you finished?" Alisha asked Carmen with pressed lips.

"Yeah, why?"

"Because I'm not.

"Well excuse the hell outta me." Carmen said with her eyes closed and rolling her neck as if she just turned ghetto fabulous.

Alisha rolled her eyes back at Carmen. "Um, before I was rudely interrupted, I was trying to tell you that there's also three hundred and nine cards and from the looks of it, everyone in this stack is balling outta control."

She picked up a stack of business cards, then slowly flipped through them like a deck of cards as she read the occupations.

"William Jacobi Law Firm, Paul & Paul Petroleum, McCrea Private Medical Practice, Bugatti Dealers, Bryson Investors, Tall Money Records, and the list goes on. Oh and by the way, there's also a note and a check for a thousand dollars."

I was wired up by hearing the large number of business cards but still showing no emotions. When it comes to pimping, imperturbability is critical, but I was good because my staying solid training run's on automatic. I kept my focus but at the same time I had to get to the bottom of this other shit that wasn't part of the play. I asked Alisha.

"What does the note say and a check from who?"

Alisha cleared her throat then said. "Well the note says: Alisha I would like to meet you in a private encounter, I will make it worthwhile. You will find a down payment. SN."

She scratched her head with her fingernail then continued. "I'm guessing the check is from the same fool because it's made out to me from Sean Nutter. Do you think it's a valid check?"

"See if he left a card." I said. "And if so, what's his line of work?"

Alisha enthusiastically flipped through the business cards until she froze, read the card then said, "Yup, Dr. Sean Nutter, Physician Plastic Surgeon MD."

"The check is valid." I said, but Carmen couldn't believe it. She threw her arms up in the air as if what she just heard was a little too far-fetched for her ears.

"Are you fucking kidding me?" Carmen said. "That means you made three thousand dollars in one night. That's impossible, like who does that?"

"Obviously I do bitch, so you might as well stop hating. I can't help it that niggas be fiending for this pussy. I mean it's not my fault, not technically."

As Carmen slowly shook her head, she said, "That was so unimportant Alisha!"

My shit hasn't even jumped off yet and these tricks are

already throwing money around as if they have no regard for the stability and value of the paper currency. But like they always said: One man's trash is the next nigga's come up.

Later that night I waited for the girls to nod out so I could do a background check on this dude. Besides, I didn't want them seeing me do this Google Search shit, whereas they'll coincidental come to think that this is the shit to do. I do it not only for war but also for social psychological research, which inevitably means forming relationships with people. This way I can, beforehand be aware of who I'm dealing with. Which is absolutely necessary for understanding the trick beyond his social status, career, money and clean cut decorations that perhaps blind the average motherfucker in thinking that they're dealing with someone sane.

Just as I thought, Sean Nutter has a checkered past. In 1996 he found himself caught up in a scandal where he was accused of having sexual relations with a Houston based, highly known prostitute; Candis 'Candy' Gainsborough. But, see, where the problem came is when he was also accused of trading surgical procedures for sex with more than a few of Candy's underage protégées. The case was eventually thrown out due to lack of evidence, but still he lost a lot of shit in the process.

Including a Bel air home, luxury vehicles, property, half his loot, his three children and his prize winning dogs to a vengeful wife.

As far as his medical practice, most of his bookings come from Houston but he is Beaumont's most in demand plastic surgeon. You would think his career would reposition in a darker light due to his background, but dig, as long as he's making clean incisions, a bitch could care less about his perversions.

By the time Carmen was elbow deep in computer detail the next morning, I was coaching Alisha proper etiquettes in dealing with rich people. At Player's all she had to do was smile and look pretty on a pole. She didn't have intimate contact with the clientele like most strippers who were required to work the floor. I showed her how to deliver a flirtatious speech and how to find her inner voice while communicating with wealth.

When it comes to opening doors, sex sells. Well at least sex appeal does. Physical and social attractiveness is an important appeal that most psychologist deem as 'Erotic Capital' and its most definitely something that the rich and wealthy is always on the hunt for.

After our first session of training we checked on Carmen to see how things were coming along. I knew her project was going in the right direction from the get go because she had a kool aid smile on her face when we stepped in the room.

She quickly turned around from the monitor screen then said, "I think I got it." She released a heavy sigh, wiped her forehead then said, "Seriously it took me like forever to make the PayPal link but I finally figured it out. Okay, tell me how it sounds and be honest, okay?"

Alisha and I grabbed both chairs from the other two desk. We scuffed our chairs closer to Carmen, then I said, "Take off, let me see what you got."

Carmen turned around towards the monitor screen, cleared her throat, then said, "Presented by Threat To The World Entertainment, you have been nominated to become an elite member of an exclusive circle of sex and friends. Where, here your sexual fantasies will become reality. This is your opportunity to connect with an underground world of complete pleasure. So come and experience the thrill and exhilaration of meeting hot, exotic girls who are open minded, willing and ready to experience this new and exciting world together. Event begins next Saturday, August 8, 2015 at 8 PM until. This is an upscale, formal attire which includes the finest champagnes, delicious catered food, poolside entertainment, indoor and outdoor sex of any exotic girl that your lusting eyes desire. Event features the wonderful Alisha Farrell and platinum blond, Carmen Styles and of course several other attractive beauties to choose from. Deposit one thousand dollars to the account number you see attached to this ecard. You can left click the link to make payment payable to Threat To The World Entertainment. Once payment is deposited, you will receive a membership number and the discrete location. Don't keep us waiting; connect and let's play."

Tilting her head to the side while staring at the monitor screen; in an uncertain tone, Carmen asked. "Or should I say presented by Threat To The World Entertainment last instead of opening?"

"What do you think?" I asked Carmen.

"I mean, I sort of like it in the opening because it gives it a jagged surface at the beginning and it's ironed out with unrestricted fantasies that I know most guys crave."

"Well there's goes your answer." I said. "As long as you like it then it's written in stone. This is your project, you and you alone is in full control of it...And its outcome! So if no one accepts our invitations then we know who to blame."

"Oh see now, that's just wrong." Carmen said. "What if they see the thousand dollar price tag and think we've gone off the rails?"

This kind of pessimistic way of thinking runs my blood hot every time. But yet I can dig it. Throughout my studies I learnt that depressed people were pessimistic about the future, and nondepressed people are optimistic. Depressed people predicted they would more likely fail than other people similar to them. on the flip side, nondepressed people predicted they would more likely succeed than other people similar to them. Optimism rises to the top because it maintains reasonable confidence that what is wanted can be had. Over the last several thousand years, techniques have been laid down to help muthafuckers condition their thoughts in ways that lead to winning. According to the laws of attraction the plan is To Be and it is, Claim it and own it, Say it and it is done. Unlike the pessimist who think winning is unrealistic. I came up with an example then asked Carmen.

"Did you see that movie 'Indecent Proposal', with Demi Moore and what's ol boy name?"

"Woody Harrelson!" Alisha said with confidence.

"Yeah, him" I said. "The same cat that stared in White Men Can't Jump. Anyway, their lives was unexpectedly interrupted by a baller who knew the worth of that pussy...

A million dollars. A million dollars is an outrageous proposal for a piece of pussy right? Especially if you're rich and you can get the shit anywhere. But is it a reasonable offer to a young couple who's madly in love? Carmen, you have to know when to raise the bar. Most of all, you have to know your worth. Are you worth fifty or sixty bucks, or even a hundred or a couple hundred not worth mentioning dollars for a complete stranger to come shove his dick in your mouth? Believe me, the rich and wealthy do not mind paying for shit with a stiff price tag. The higher it is only appreciates it's worth. So tell me this. Why do you have a problem demanding it?"

Carmen sat there looking dumbfounded while Alisha had a devilish smirk on her face. I wanted them to marinate on what I just said so I decided to fall back. Life was good and the dream is alive. But still it was a house of cards, and any number of bad luck or bad timing scenarios could send this shit crashing down. At this point there was one important matter that had my personal concern and it had to be taken care of now before it slipped to far into the week. Only a bottom bitch could make it happen. Only a bottom bitch would even be motivated to make it happen. Only a bottom bitch would 'Be With It' when a pimp is in high pursuit of a prostitute. Before I left the computer room, I said, "Hey Alisha!"

"What's up Daddy?"

"Find more hoes. ASAP!"

CHAPTER 13
DIAMOND IN A ROUGH

Monday morning started with a seven mile run to Orange, where I found a 24 hour fitness center; The King's Gym. On the spot I paid for a year's membership and dove right into a high intense interval training full body workout. I crunk it up with a cardio regimen of sparing with the bag, jump rope, a 30 degree incline run on the treadmill and a high rep circuit routine with dips, leg ups and vertical jumps with no rest in between sets. On the weights I started off using light weights at a high volume of sets and then progressed to heavy weights at a low volume. I went around the world with squats, presses, rows, weighted chin ups, deadlifts, and all other variations.

Again, eyeballs were beamed in my direction, but as twisted as it may sound, I was getting use to the shit. A bad built nigga was there with what it appeared to be his wife. While he was giving her a spot from behind on the military press, she kept her eyes locked in on my every movement. I could only imagine what she was thinking but the nigga's eyes were locked in too and it was kind of eerie trying to picture what he was thinking. But dig, I didn't trip, I just put on a show with an amplified workout that called for exaggerated strains, overemphasized movements and not one time wiping my sweat. I wanted my body to shine and glisten so it could complement my rock hard abs, my ripped and pumped up muscles and my flawless skin so this nigga and his looking ass wife can clearly see that I'm setting the standard for all the bad built niggas in this city. Step your game up or else your bitch is coming home with me.

While I was jogging home and when I eventually made it to the street that lead to my house, I slowed down almost to a complete stop. I was halfway down the street and according to my watch, I been running for a quarter mile from the main street. So the street is at least a half mile stretch. I thought how proper the street would be to accommodate parking. Cars could simply parallel park and no doubt fit on both sides. Everything is falling in place like pieces to a puzzle, which brought to mind a Steve Jobs quote: Creativity is just connecting things.

Just as I was approaching the circle driveway, Alisha pulled up in the Camaro with someone on the passenger's side. Alisha was looking proper as usual with army fatigue boy shorts, a black wife beater overlapping a fatigue bathing suit top. She was also rocking an army fatigue bandana that was propping up her curly hair and on her feet she had on black low top patent leather Prada sneakers. But when the girl on the passenger's side stepped out of the Camaro, my head jerked back as I thought: What the fuck?

The bitch looked like some shit straight outta a Michael Jackson Thriller video. I bugged at the whole scene. She had on an old beat up yellow T-shirt that was possibly four sizes too big for her lanky body frame. She was wearing baggy black slacks that sagged in the crotch area, which reminded me of MC Hammer parachute pants. And on her feet she had on purple beachcomber flip flops. Her hair was dark and long but dull and flat. It looked like she found a mop, spray painted it black, then slapped that bitch on top her head. She had dirt smeared from one side of her face to the other, so it was difficult to distinguish her nationality. I couldn't tell if she was Mexican, Puerto Rican, Arab or what.

Alisha didn't look back, nor did she acknowledge me. She just lead the homeless looking chick through the front and left the door wide open, which was her way of reassuring me that she knew I was in the vicinity. I noticed them carrying a couple of boxes of champagne and it was a magnificent sight,seeing my bitch already on top of shit. When I stepped in the door I walked right pass them and was smacked in the face with a reeking odor that bore the scent of a wet dog. This bitch best keep it standing because if she so far as think to sit on my brand new couch, then I'm gonna catch a brand new case.

I could see through the corner of my eye that they were following me to the kitchen. I kept my back to them while I opened the refrigerator door. I reached deep to the back so I could get my hands on the muscle milk protein shake I needed to fuel my muscles. With the refrigerator door still open, I turned the muscle milk bottle up towards the ceiling and washed the 26 grams of protein down in maybe three to four swallows. When I turned around they both were standing there; Alisha with her arms crossed over her breast, looking like a sexy version of G.I. Jane and the bum, refugee looking chick had her head down looking pitiful as hell. I slammed the bottle into the counter top on the island, then asked Alisha.

"Where the fuck you find this bum looking bitch?"

"Who the fuck you talking to, nigga you don't know me like that?" The chick said with her eyes closed and her right hand on her hip. Alisha shot back quick with a raised hand and jerky head movements.

"Uh.uh bitch, you better watch your trap before I slap the taste out yo mouth. Now shut the fuck up. I told you to let me do the talking hoe. What part of that do you not understand? Show some respect in this house or get a beat down. A matter fact, take that ass to the living room." Alisha said with her index finger pointed towards the living room's direction. The chick didn't say shit, she just smacked her lips, rolled her eyes then stormed that way. She walked away so fast, all I heard were her flip flops flapping against her soles. But before she made it to the archway, Alisha said, "And don't touch shit either. Stay standing until I come get you."

I never seen Alisha go that way but I got to admit, it was hella sexy seeing her bossed up and holding the purse strings over a bitch. Also it somewhat boosted my thirst to make sense of what exactly she had jumping. But she threw me for a loop with the sudden out of the blue mood change. She switched gears faster than Maya or better yet, the crazy bitch from that movie Misery.

Like presto, she was someone else. She walked over to me with a slight pout in her bottom lip. She gazed up at me with her hypnotic eyes that were softening with her stare. She was rubbing her arm as if it were a jinni bottle and it was going to grant her wish. With a soft tone she said; "Daddy please, you have to look deep. There's a surprise hidden beneath the dirt. Just use your artistic eye and you'll see that she has potential."

"Potential for what?" I asked with a quick widening of my eyes.

"To work for us, for you. She's young and barely touched. She will work out fine, trust. I will take full responsibility and work with her until she gets the hang of things.

Alisha stood there staring up at me on standby, anticipating my response. I stood with a solid confrontational stance with my mind racing through all the possible things that could backfire. I was clinched to the flaws, both logic and the physical nature of the situation. But there were two major questions that had to be answered before we could press forward.

I asked Alisha, "Is she on drugs? And how old is the little girl, she looks like she's in middle school or something. You know damn well I don't rock with the adolescent shit. Show me some I.D. or get the bitch the fuck up outta here."

"She was, yes" Alisha said. "She's kicking the habit. But she's just being rebellious against her family right now by living on the street. She's actually from Oklahoma and yup, she does have a I.D.

Alisha was thrilled to show me the I.D. She whipped it out from her army boy shorts where she had it concealed to her waist line like a pistol. She sat it on top of the counter top where I could examine it then said, "See, her name is Tabatha Sixshooter. She was born September of 1996, which means she'll be 19 next month. She's full blood Native American and she and her whole family is from Oklahoma. She's only been on the streets for a couple of months. I'm telling you daddy that we can rescue her before she's too far gone."

"Excuse me y'all." Tabatha interrupted from the archway.

"I thought I told you to,

"It's good Alisha." I said with my arm thrust forward. Then I switched my attention to Tabatha.

"What's poppin shorty? Introduce yourself and tell me what you got."

Tabatha made eye contact with Alisha, at the same time Alisha nodded her head one solid time, giving her the green light to press on. Tabatha looked like she was going through an erratic thought process with irrational fears. She was fidgeting with short twitching movements and flexing her fingers while curling and uncurling them.

She cleared her throat, peered her eyes up towards the ceiling then said, "Um, my name is Tabatha; Tabatha Sixshooter. I'm Cherokee Indian and I'm from the Cherokee strip in Oklahoma. Um, I'm 19, well I'll be 19 next month. I'm flexible, I mean I can work full time. I really need to get off the streets but I ain't trying to go back to my family. But I know a few things and if you give me another chance, I can prove it to you. My bad for jumping off at the mouth. I'm just stressed out right now. But um, I can do better, I swear on the bible."

I was cracking up on the inside but still showing no sign of amusement. I was beginning to catch a glimpse of what Alisha envisioned. Regardless of her filth, ragged out clothes and reeking odor, I saw a sign. It was right there in front of my face. I can't call it why I didn't peep it at first glance. How did I fall short to notice that the bitch had perfect teeth.

I like to consider my long distance vision like an eagle and my optics like an owl because I can see ten times what normal niggas don't see and twice as better at night. But see, I wasn't beating myself up that Alisha saw something that I didn't because after all, that's what bottom bitches are for; to pick up on what a pimp missed.

Carmen came prancing in the kitchen barefooted with her eyes glued to her cell phone. You could tell she was caught up with her project because she was still unaware that there were three people in the kitchen when she stepped in. She had on boy shorts too but only hers were red with two white stripes traveling down both sides. She also had on a white wife beater without a bra so her extra-large titties and protruding nipples were trying to escape from her shirt. At last, Carmen realized that she was on stage. She took a quick glimpse at everyone and I guess from a women's intuition she must have sensed tension in the air. She froze with a slow stiff rotation, she asked.

"What's going on?"

"We have another project." Alisha said. Then she pointed at Tabatha. "We're going to do a makeover with that!"

Carmen looked at Tabatha with her chin ducked to her neck. Her mouth fell open without words coming out. Then finally she said, "Oh really?"

I fell back and took a shower downstairs in the guest bath- room while they occupied the master bedroom and pretty much the entire second story of the house. I could hear footsteps above my head running back and forth with accelerated speed as if they were a crew team at a NASCAR pit stop. I glanced upwards at the ceiling and I could only imagine Tabatha sitting there while Alisha and Carmen took charge of her life in full: "Wear this, no put this on. Lay back. Be still. Turn this way. How does this look Carmen?" Not once will they ask Tabatha's opinion because she has no say so. She's now held hostage to Alisha and Carmen's beck and call.

I shut the door and sat peaceful in the computer room where I stared at my old man's picture. At the time of this picture he had seven hoes, all dimes and a party mix of varieties. A Latina, blonds, a freckle face chick with red hair, a couple of jet black chocolate crows that looked like they could melt in your mouth and he even had an Asian persuasion on the team. Now that's what's up; a lil sumpin sumpin for everybody.

My old man had taste and he most definitely had style. He wasn't the typical pimp nigga of the 70's and 80's era with butterfly collars, bellbottoms, mink coats, platform shoes, large hats and clown suits. No sir, my dude was tailor made and fashionably fitted in either French or Italian designer suits imported straight from Sicily or Valle D' Aosta. He wore the finest threads and stayed sharp as a razor in gators, Stacy Addams or Cole Haan's. His jewelry stayed elegant and tasteful with one diamond pinky ring and two gold heron bones with an iced out pendant that exhibited the initials P.I.

While I was sitting there with my feet cocked up, relaxed, chilling and mesmerized by my old man's lifestyle, I get a ring on my cell. It was a 214 area code and straight up off the top I thought who in the hell could be calling me from Dallas. I was slack answering the call but quick peeping who it was. As soon as I heard the voice, lo and behold, Mack was on the other line.

"What you know young blood? Now don't you go asking a million questions how I got your number. If you pay bills then your number is gonna be listed in the white pages online. Privacy is something of the past son."

I chuckled then said. "All man, no stress. It's live hearing from you; what's been up?"

"Well you know me, I got my hands on a few things and a couple other projects in the making but nothing final. Been working on a book but a few players ain't feeling me exposing the game on that level. Oh, and I read all your books by the way. You got yourself a natural gift son. I knew you had it in you. But how you been holding up?"

"Living the dream baby." I said. "I got a few things in the making myself big pimpin. I'm two strong with a possible."

"Is the bottom foundation laid down solid?"

"Solid as a rock!"

"Well then you're on your way young blood. just remember not to get comfortable in one spot because you got the whole world to work with. International, cross country is the only way son."

"I can check for that." I said. "Look, I just want to thank you big pimpin for taking me under your wing and lacing my mental up to what I needed to do in order to win. I knew exactly what you were talking about. All you had to do was plant the seed."

All at once there was an unexpected silence on the line. I could tell Mack was in a restaurant or something because I could hear faded chatter, clinking plates and elevator music in the background. I could hear him sipping from his drink, then he said, "You sound pretty solid, like you playing with a full deck. Word on the street, you thought you were Superman at your last unit. Them crackers didn't put you on they psych load did they?"

I cracked up laughing. "Nah big pimpin, I got a royal flush. As a matter fact, I mastered the science of the mind, the science of the human behavior and any other human thought process. If anything, they need to be coming to ya man for psychotherapy."

We cracked up, rejoiced and tossed up ideas with each other in codes to where we were the only ones who could interpret what we were stressing. I mean I did that to satisfy him because I'm convinced that there's nothing slick under the sun that hasn't already been exposed. But on the flip side, I felt out of line for not lacing Mack up about the voices I been hearing. I was exploring this from all angles;

particularly dogma, power and manipulation. But at the same time, what he don't know won't complicate shit. Besides, it's just a minor glitch that will sooner or later be placed on ice. The voices calling my name will no doubt fade away.

But dig, when we disconnected I was all smiles and in a zone of vibes. Not in an emotional state but on a first class trip to positive thinking. I was at ease with the world and all the player shit that came with it. In my mind I was doing victory laps around the hard knocks that lead to this moment. Yeah, all the while with two fist thrusted in the sky. I knew I was going to win. I felt like Neo in the Matrix. I was specifically chosen, exclusively called upon to take this game to a whole different level. After talking to my dude Mack, it's official. I'M A MUTHAFUCKING PIMP!

Out of the blue my phone started blowing up. I was able to catch the call from Urma though. We had a full fledge conversation in Spanish and off the top I noticed that she was trying to pick my brain, you know; feel me out type of shit. After a 30 minute conversation, she said that she could not live at the house because she has a husband and six ninos to look after, but she could work long hours every day, with the exception of Sunday's due to Catholic Mas. I told her that I could pay her twice what she made at the La Quinta Inn and without thinking twice, she said, "When can I start?"

I told her whenever she felt like making some money but I absolutely needed her before this weekend. I had two voice mails; one from Maya and another one from a number that I didn't recognize. I listened to Maya's first;

"What's up big pimpin?" Maya giggled at her own statement. "But anyway, I was going to surprise you with something. You know me, I'm full of surprises right? Well, I'm just gonna flat out tell you because your new lifestyle is a tad bit unpredictable for my blood pressure. I swear you're doing the most and I don't want to pop up on something that I don't intend to see. Images are hard to remove from your brain you know? Anyway, I just wanted to let you know that Edwin will be in town next week and to be completely honest with you, I think he's gonna pop the question Threat, I can feel it in my bones. I'm sooo nervous. Seriously though, I will definitely tell you details. Cross your fingers for me okay? Love ya big bro; oh I mean big pimpin."

Maya laughed again as I skipped to the next voice mail; "I don't know what you want from me but you need to know that I am not a whore. It's quite obvious that you are a pimp. I'm just saying, you stand out like a sore thumb. But if you ever have entertainment like a banquet, celebration or a formal dinner that needs cocktails catered, then give me a call. Other than that, please do not expect anything else." Beep.

I was bugging at the last voicemail, trying to figure out who the fuck it was. Then a lightbulb lit up inside my dome. It was the waitress from Player's. Shanna, the chocolate delight bitch who suffered the delusion that her shit don't stink. But it's all live because now she was peeping inside the world of a pimp. What, you think you can knock on the devil's door and he ain't gonna answer?

Speaking of knocking on someone's door; I was brought back to earth with loud knocking on the computer room's door. I glanced at the clock and was tripping to see that almost three hours passed since I been chillin in here.

"Threat c'mon open up, Pleaaaase."

"Hold up!" I said as I was approaching the door. Before I opened the door, I heard a whisper.

"Here he comes."

When I opened the door, Carmen was standing there with her arms stretched wide, creating a wall so I couldn't see what was behind her. I heard Alisha say, "Make sure he can't see."

That's when Carmen blindfolded me with her hand while she lead the way to the formal living room. By the time we were next to the couch, Carmen gradually removed her hand from my face saying.

"Keep your eyes shut, do not open them yet."

I could smell the fragrance of a woman's perfume. It smelt sweet and pure with a fresh aromatic savory to it. I could even smell hints of shampoo which forced me to get a good whiff. I inhaled the whole atmosphere, then released it with a smirk on my face.

"Can I open them now?" I asked while I heard Alisha and Carmen countdown in unison.

"Five. Four. Three. Two. One." Carmen said. "We introduce to you, Tabatha Sixshooter."

When I opened my eyes I was blew back like a 'Goddamn' type of way. I made eye contact with Alisha and she nodded her head as to say: Yup, it's the same girl. I was staring at a metamorphism right now. Tabatha transformed from a zombie into a Cherokee goddess. She wore an open red silk robe that reached to her waistline. Other than that she was standing there in her birthday suit with six inch high heels with a strap that wrapped around her ankles and stopped at mid-point before reaching her calf muscles. Her skin was olive with a hint of lemon. Her dark eyes were both wise and youthful and she was blessed with an incredible petite body. On the real, she was looking like a Victoria's Secret Angel right now. Her pussy hairs were neatly trimmed in a race track design that was en route towards her flat stomach. Her small titties were shaped like mangos but her nipples were long and hard, standing perpendicular for attention. The dirt is now cleansed from her face so you can clearly see her high cheekbones, her bold and broad features from her Indian heritage. She had Alisha's signature written all over her with pink French tip finger and matching toenails. She had heavy mascaraed eyes, trimmed eyebrows and her lips was popping with lip gloss. She had an Egyptian blunt cut with bangs running straight across her forehead and the rest of her long hair was lying flat on her back. Damn, Alisha is a fucking genius because I had my eyes on a dime right now.

I stared deep into Tabatha's dark round eyes. She beamed back with narrowing eyes and an intense focus. I could tell that her self-esteem and confidence sky rocketed because she had a sense of calm and ease. Her posture was relaxed and her chin was high. I asked her.

"So you ready to get down with the team?"

Tabatha was most definitely feeling herself because she gracefully shook her hair from left to right. With her chin high, she said, "Yup, I sure am."

When she spoke, her perfect pearly white teeth sparkled. With her mouth half opened, she grazed her tongue slowly across her teeth then asked.

"What do I have to do?"

"What you need 'Not' to do is drugs because if I catch you so far as popping an ibuprofen then your ass is gonna be up outta here quicker than you came in, feel me?"
She nodded her head, then said. "That's A ok with me because I'm all in with dope. It's really not my thing."

"This here is a money making stable of nothing but greatness and success" I said. "Tell me this: How can you contribute to the cause?"

Tabatha walked straight over to me with a flirtatious strut. Her red silk robe swayed behind her while her naked body lead the way. When she entered my space, she looked up at me with her dark bedroom eyes, she said, "I listen well."

I couldn't contain the smirk that was building up on my face; and to keep it hella real, I couldn't contain my dick from rocking up either.

"That's what's up!"

I looked at Alisha then said. "Go get a bottle and four glasses, it's time to celebrate."

Alisha took off towards the kitchen but Carmen suddenly splayed her hands out wide to stretch, then relaxed them again. I caught on quick that the only reason she done that shit was to be noticed. She wanted something to do. So I said, "Carmen go get a condom."

She took off in a chop chop manner while two minutes

later Alisha pulled up with an open bottle of Dom Perignon, four champagne glasses and four marble coasters resting on a silver platter. She sat the platter down on the table as Carmen came rushing in with the condom wrapped with a white napkin. Alisha poured a quarter of champagne in each glass then handed each of us one with a smiling face. She positioned Carmen and herself on both sides of Tabatha while Tabatha stood before me with examing eyes. I raised my glass at shoulder length and as everyone did the same, I said "We are here as a body of associates, all on the same page of money making endeavors. In this event, you Tabatha chose me to guide and protect you as we climb the ladder to success. Anything less than the top is unacceptable. I am your pimp and you are my bitch, nothing more, nothing less. You will stay in pocket, you will keep your emotions in check and I shall do the same. Nothing, no one or anything imaginable will derail this money train. This is a toast to greatness."

We made the toast, and I finished the toast with; "This is a drink to success."

When we finished the champagne, I asked Tabatha. "So you do understand that I'm now your pimp right?"

She nodded with a mumble. "MMhmm."

I stared at her calmly, waiting to hear more. Then Alisha leaned over to whisper in her ear.

"You have to say Threat or daddy with a clear yes or no."

Tabatha cleared her throat. "Yes daddy. Threat, I'm with that."

"Do you know the prime and number one reason why

you're on this team?"

"No, not really."

I reached my hand out for the condom and as Carmen placed it in my right hand, I said, "Because I dig your name."

I gave Tabatha the condom then said. "Put it on my dick."

Tabatha squatted down to a lower positon while loosening my belt to my slacks. She kept her bedroom eyes locked in on me the whole time. She unzipped my pants and slowly dropped them, including my boxers down to my ankles. She tore the condom package with her teeth while stroking my dick until it was in full length. Then she put the condom in her mouth and just like a magic trick, she rolled the condom down my dick with her mouth. I pulled her up, turned her around and right before I made penetration, Carmen and Alisha was spreading Tabatha's ass cheeks apart so I could easily slide in.

I wrapped my hand with her long jet black hair, pulled her closer to me then entered her tight pussy from the back strong and hard. Her little ass took all twelve inches while I fucked her as if I was mad at her. She threw that ass back at me with a beautiful arch. I reached my hand out again and Alisha read the play. She put the Dom Perignon bottle in my hand while my pelvis and hips were moving a hundred miles per hour. My body slapping against her ass was powerful and thundering. My grip to her hair strengthened. My teeth gritted. Tendons stretched from my neck.

I'm going harder. I'm going faster. I poured the bottle of Dom over her head and all over her entire body. She rejoiced with her mouth open. Her arms reached out to the ceiling. She's loving it. She moaned. She screamed. She's cumming. She spoke in tongues as she yelled out to the heavens.

"Oh, oh, yes, yes, Threat, daddy, daddy, I'm yours."

CHAPTER 14
OUT OF POCKET

I'm what most muthafuckers like to call well endowed. Bitches like that. It gives them a de facto sense of power knowing that they have something special. On the other hand, there are people who actually believe that it isn't the size of the boat but the motion of the ocean. Come on now. Any bitch who tells you that size doesn't matter is only gassing you up with lies; maybe to spare your feelings. I know this shit because all three of my hoes were fiending for the dick all night long.

Tabatha's pussy is tighter than frog pussy and still no complaints. She took it like a vet and Alisha and Carmen were looking forward to their turn as if they were junkies waiting on a fix. They were strung out. You could even see it in their facial expressions when I fucked Tabatha. Their spellbound eyes was gazed in on my dick while I was going in and out of her. Alisha frequently sucked air through her teeth and Carmen seductively licked her lips. They couldn't wait any longer so I gave them what they wanted but still sucking Tabatha's perky little titties at the same damn time.

Tuesday morning the curtains were open so the sunrise naturally woke everyone up. The sound of bluebirds chirping on the balcony was in perfect harmony and just about the right blend with the sunrise outlined a perfect morning. Yeah, even despite the fact that there were female hormones and emotions all over the place, it was still a beautiful day in Little Cypress.

I woke up with Tabatha buried in my chest and Carmen on the right side of the bed staring at the ceiling. Alisha was at the foot of the bed with her arms crossed with tightness in her expression and jumping to conclusions.

"So I guess Tabatha took our place huh?"

Alisha asked with a hint of sarcasm but still looking for ways to become argumentive. Carmen turned her head my way as if she was on plex mode too. They were searching for answers because they didn't see Tabatha laid up in my chest and wrapped up in my arms as kosher to the plan. That's some twisted shit because this is the same girl that came up in here tore up from the floor up and was looking so bad that she made the Zombie Apocalypse look decent. Now she got my hoes paranoid. Or, maybe it's the Dick? I been sticking it to them hard, long and strong that now it got their equilibrium off balance. Bottom line is, these hoes are out of pocket. I told Alisha.

"I think it would be wise to keep that tude in check, know what I mean?"

"I ain't tripping." Alisha said. "I just wish I could lay up under you like that. I tried to the first night we all got down but you pushed me off so I just left it alone."

Tabatha pulled the heavy comforter from her naked

body, sat up then said through a stretching yawn.

"We can switch places Alisha, I don't wanna cause no problems."

Through gritted teeth, Alisha said. "I don't think I was talking to you Tabatha. Stay in your lane little girl."

"Stay in my lane?"

"Yeah hoe, you heard what I said, did I stutter?"

Carmen has mastered a strategy in disappearing when shit is about to get thick. I looked up and all I seen was her naked white ass cheeks vanishing from the bedroom. But dig, I can't blame her though because this was beginning to develop into one of those 'Fight or Flight' situations. So, if you really ain't bout that life, then the best thing you should do is fall back while you can. Nevertheless, I knew I had to put a fire extinguisher to this blaze before it grew like a wild fire. We got shit to do, people to call, people to see, know what I mean?

Alisha and Tabatha were heated and staring at each other as if they were just waiting for someone to bust a move. I was also getting a little tight myself and truth be told, I wanted to give the both of them a hellacious pimp slap, but I knew better than to react with emotion. Besides, I knew what I had to do.

Like a hangover, I had to fix the problem with what caused the problem. You know, the hair of the dog that bit you? I paused, counted backwards from ten, exhaled, then said,

"Alisha get up here."

She pouted as she scooted closer to Tabatha. When she came close enough for arms reach, I positioned her face to face with Tabatha. At this point both of their nostrils were flaring and Tabatha was holding her elbows wide from her body with her little titties thrusted out. I could tell that Alisha's body was tensed up and she was trying to control herself by flexing her fingers. I also knew that any sudden movement from Tabatha would get her ass kicked. So I quickly said.

"Now kiss and make up."

"What?" Alisha asked with a double take at me.

"You heard what I said, kiss and make up. It's not an option Alisha."

Alisha smacked her lips and rolled her eyes as if she were a shorty who was just ordered to go to her room. Tabatha tilted her head to the side with pursed lips as if she were asking Alisha, "Well?" Alisha looked at me again with a long face.

"Do I have to?

"You fucking right you have to." I said with a solid tone. "We got shit to do and money to make and you sitting up here lolly-gagging and pussyfooting around with these juvenile emotions that you suppose that have wrapped tight. You my bottom bitch, you supposed to be setting an example for any bitch that even considers getting outta pocket, feel me? You the one who upgraded Tabatha, now you want to destroy her? You the one who convinced me to notice her potentials, so now what; you want me to camouflage what I see? Then you got the muthafucking audacity to ask me if you have to? This is the type of..."

Before I could say another word, Alisha was kissing Tabatha. Not a peck on the cheek or a mere nibble on the lips. No sir, I'm talking about a closed eyes, tongue swapping, wet, passionate kiss that encouraged my dick to rise for the occasion. I had to 'Put On' with a bogus attitude because I felt like Alisha was testing me to see where I was at. Hoes are artful at playing games and crafty in being devious so sometimes you have to play them at their own game.

I broke off their inviting kiss and while Tabatha's eyes were halfway open, I nodded my head for her to get out of the bedroom. I saw a hesitation, it was hardly noticeable but enough for me to raise my eyebrows to the point where she knew I meant now.

Tabatha quietly closed the door behind her and when I knew she was far away from the scene, I fucked Alisha one on one without any interruptions. To top it off, I even ate her pussy. No bitch is this entire world can tell you the same.

Alisha woke up this morning feeling territorial like a goddamn monkey. This holds weight considering the fact that women are 99% emotion and 1% rational. In the real world, nothing is gonna go smooth sailing when you're dealing with a house full of pussy. No ifs ands or buts about it, shit is gonna go down regardless of your rules, regulations or creeds. It's already prescribed to you for the lifestyle you embarked on. So it's like this, you can deal with it like a bitch would and react with emotions, or you can use your intellect, creativity, sound judgment and do whatever it takes to gain control. I choose the later with my big dick slapped right on top of it like icing on a cake. And you know what? I haven't had a problem out of Alisha for the rest of the day. She sets the tone for every bitch in this house, and at this particular time there's nothing but high energy, smiles, giggling and laughter that shows no sign of pulling up. Yeah, while I'm giving myself a gang of mental high fives.

CHAPTER 15
SECRETS TO SUCCESS

Wednesday jumped off on a better note with progressive actions towards our goals. Alisha cashed the thousand dollar check and used the additional two thousand dollars to buy basic essentials and a list I gave her for the alcohol I needed her to get for the party. She also took Tabatha to the mall and jazzed her wardrobe up with a few designer clothes and a couple gold accessories. To sum it up, Alisha and Tabatha basically had a girls day out.

Tabatha's nails and toes were now professionally on point with fly designs and a clear coated gloss. She had on white Nicholas Kirkwood peep toe shoes, a black Marc Jacob mini skirt, showcasing her slim and defined legs and a black and white slim fitted T-shirt with 'Team Threat' written on the front. Alisha proudly rocked the same T-shirt and it felt superior seeing my hoes representing on a grandstand level.

I helped them unload the bags and an umpteen amount

of boxes from the Camaro. As we were putting everything on top of the kitchen's island top, Alisha said, "I went to the liquor store on 16th and they were stocked with almost everything you had on the list. I got the St. George Californa Agricole rum, the Black Rock Barbados rum and all the vodkas and gins you wanted too. I had to go to Beaumont to get the martini mix and more Dom though. While I was there I went ahead and got some Silver Patron tequila, Cognac and red and white wines that the clerk suggested."

"Did you get the party essentials?" I asked Alisha while I was investigating the bags.

"I did!" Alisha said. She opened one of the boxes that had the words 'Novelty Dreams' written on it. She brought out a white mask and said, "At the novelty shop they had a Mardi Gras section with these mask. You have no idea what we had to go through to get 300 of these."

Tabatha was putting a ham and cheese hot pocket in the microwave and she was making it obviously clear that she's comfortably at home. She said, "Oh you talking about Mr. Nigga Please."

They both cracked up laughing and when Alisha regained her composure, she said, "The sales person was some crusty African nigga asking us a million and two questions. What is your nationality? Is this to be your sister? What is your age? Blaze, blaze. But then Kunta kente asked me, do you have marriage to a man? I'm like, uh, Yeah! But I played it off and told him no because I needed him to hustle up 300 of these mask. There wasn't nothing but sixteen on the shelf. So when I told him I was looking for a hardworking man and that I needed 300 of these mask, he shot off like a rocket to the back. Five minutes later he came back with all these damn boxes. He said that there's more than 300 mask, which he called dominos by the way. He said he would get in the most of trouble for selling them to one customer. I told him, "Shit then don't sell them." And don't you know we walked right out the front door without paying for the boxes and the rest of the shit we needed too? He stopped me when we came for the last box. He asked me, "What is your name?" When me and Tabatha was finally leaving, we said at the same time: NIGGA PLEASE!"

They laughed again except this time a little harder. Alisha laughed so hard it became soundless and Tabatha turned away to collect herself so she didn't choke on her hot pocket. I didn't trip though because it demonstrated their ability to work together as a team. Besides, it was live seeing my hoes bonding instead of hackled up like two aggravated cats. They linked up on some African nigga and in the process, they read each other's energy and communicated without saying a word. And, when they did finally speak, they spoke in union. Nigga Please!

Most foreigners are open mouthed fascinated by the American pussy. When it comes to pussy period, they lose their course of thought and make moronic judgments. They still don't get it and I know it sounds like a cliché, you know what I'm saying, but money on the real, cannot buy love.

Although I suppose it can buy a piece of pussy for a few hours though. Likewise, I ain't mad at them either because their infatuations and obsessions becomes my trip to the bank. How in the hell can I be mad at a contributor to the game? Out of nowhere Carmen came running in the kitchen, screaming at the top of her lungs. She was extra animated and we were her audience. She bottled up her breath to try an effort at calming down. Then as she exhaled, she dragged her words out.

"Everyone...come to the computer room."

Carmen now had her blond hair slicked back in a ponytail and rolled up into a bun at the back of her head. She had her ear- piece on, red eye glasses halfway down the bridge of her nose and you could tell she was feeling her position as computer detail.

Everyone stared at her as if she just lost her damn mind but evidently she didn't care. She simply aimed her index finger at us, turned her hand around, then repeatedly curled her finger as if she were saying 'Come Here' in sign language. We trailed in behind her while Alisha and Tabatha stared at each other with open palms. Carmen continuously shot her eyes back at us as if she was a mother duck with the need to keep an eye on her chicks.

However, when we set foot in the computer room, and as soon as I shut the door behind us, she turned around facing us with her back to the desktop's monitor screen. She tugged down both sleeves to her shirt with a confident smile and a gleam in her crystal blue eyes. She stretched her arms wide then said, "Honest to God guys, I did not expect this. I know, I know; that is so not cool. Hey, I'm only telling the truth. But seriously, like I would have never thought in a million years that this many guys would send a thousand dollars to our account. When I first noticed the bank statement, all I said was, are you fucking serious? One hundred and ninety five guys already sent a thousand dollars to the account and we still have three days left until the party."

"So that means we have a hundred and ninety-five thousand dollars in the Threat To The World account?" Alisha asked.

"Yup!" Carmen said while pointing at the monitor screen. "Look for yourself, Threat is a fucking genius. Literally, like he really knows what he's doing."

"What, so you're just now convinced of that?" Tabatha asked with aggressive teasing with the intent to put Carmen in her place.

Carmen didn't find the shit funny because she aimed a wicked stare at Tabatha over the top of her red glasses. I found it necessary to muscle my way in before this stage switched into a dramatic scene.

"That's what's up Carmen." I said. "Now create a countdown clock that they can see. I'm thinking by the minute, or even by the second. This will exalt their anticipation and send their testosterone levels through the roof."

Without thinking, Carmen retreated from Tabatha and shot right back into her bubbly mode.

"Oh yeah, that sounds awesome because I'm chatting with a few of them online and they can't wait. Our inbox is full but I'm having to send a lot of emails to junk mail because some of these guys are super weird, oh my God. I mean they're really creeping me out with the Do you do greek? Is the back door open? Do you do bareback? Can I cross dress? One weirdo even had the nerve to ask me if I could wear a strap on. Ugh, I'm like seriously? I wanted to puke."

Alisha laughed. "Hey, I ain't even gonna front, I'll fuck the shit outta one of them fags. If that's what they want, shit then why not stick it to um?"

"Now that's just gross Alisha. You're nasty."

"Bitch, you don't even know the half." Alisha said. "I'm X-rated, freaky and even a little on the kinky side, but I ain't nasty. There's a difference you know?"

Alisha and Tabatha laughed then high fived each other while my mind was racing a thousand miles per hour. New doors opened, different ideas were popping up in my dome like popcorn. I was charged up like a cell phone battery with all the existing bars. I was feeling dynamic but from a 'Play For Keeps' point of view.

You have to understand that I am not in love so I analyze everything from a business perspective. Not from a holy matrimony, fire and desire, forever my lady perspective, feel me? Because if it's good for business then it's well suited for free enterprise.

Like a dog owner, you have to categorize your hoes as a good or bad breed. If you pull a hoe who's willing to flirt around with the taboo shit and is game to go along with what society considers forbidden, then you got yourself a bona fide thoroughbred. Don't think less of her either. Congratulate her, pat her on the back while you tell her 'Good Girl'. Even give her a treat or two. Now you might read between the lines and suspect what I'm stressing is inhumane. But dig, you also have to take into consideration that any female who's in my circle or up under me, overall...She's my bitch!

I focused on my bottom bitch then asked her. "Alisha, is Tabatha the only recruit you found for the party?"

"Oh shit!" Alisha said while shaking her head. "My bad, my bad, I knew I was forgetting something. I was meaning to tell you the other day, it musta slipped my mind. But, yeah, I got three of the best girls from the club. I was lucky to catch up with them before they hopped their ass on a plane to another city. And I got my home girl Maria and three other girls from Orange and them hoes are down too. Oh and trust, they are all qualified to make the cut."

Alisha giggled. "But we got to pay them hoes cause they're all like, how much he talking bout? What we gotta do? Yada yada! I told them, shit it's a lot more than them blunts and exo's y'all be fucking and sucking for. These hoes done sucked dry every Tom, Dick and Harry in Orange and still don't have shit to show for it."

"Alright, check it out." I told Alisha. "Stay in contact with them and make sure they show up here Saturday at noon sharp. Keep note of the ones who need rides so we can throw that in our schedule. Most important, if Facebook, Instagram or Twitter dominates majority of these hoes time, then make sure they don't post any of this information online. This shit is crucial Alisha so stay on top of it. Oh, and make sure they bring I.D!"

"Trust." Alisha said while nodding her head.

I turned to Tabatha, "For the next three days Alisha's going to be working with you on proper etiquettes in dealing with ballers with money. I need you on your P's and Q's because I got a project lined up for the party with your name on it. Are you down?"

"Hell to the yeah I'm down." Tabatha said while swinging her arms back and forth.

More than likely she was building the party up in her mental far beyond its reality. But it's all live because I know she's developing a compulsion to detour towards something new. Tabatha is a devoted soul and a true blue. She has a lot of heart and I know it has a lot to do with what flows through her veins. A Cherokee Indian; one of the five civilized tribes of the North American Indians. She is unquestionably a true warrior at heart and spirit. Unfortunately, she, like many other authentic bloodlines has adopted physically and psychologically to the European culture, which is better known as 'Americanized.' But dig, my mission is by far to help her identify with self because after all, it's not good for business.

On the other hand, I felt the need for lacing Carmen up with the secrets to success because she's not convinced that the laws of attraction is real. I told her.

"You are doing one hellava job Carmen. You are displaying consistency, dedication and the most enthusiasm it takes to get the project done, and I appreciate that. Take a mental note so it can become plain as day that success acknowledges hard work and diligent efforts. There's no magic wand, great illusions or hocus pocus so don't be surprised when success answers back. Welcome it as you knew it was coming in the first place. Society has made success seem like some kind of farfetched fantasy but in reality it's easy as 1, 2, 3. Look at it as opening that goddamn door right there. You know the minimal and maximum effort it's going to take in walking over there to that door. You know it's not going to open on its own when you get there. You also know that it's going to take an act of exertion of physical effort in raising your hand, turning the doorknob and subconsciously you already know the precise amount of force it's going to take in pulling that motherfucker open. Would you be surprised if it opened? No because you knew it was going to open the moment you tried. Look at success like opening a door Carmen."

I walked to the door, opened it, I looked at Carmen and said, "But the only thing is. I will be the only one opening and closing doors around here!"

CHAPTER 16
ASIAN CONNECTION

Thursday was active. After a ten-mile run, eating breakfast with the girls, showering up and flipping through the bullshit news channels, the girls and I had a meeting. We were in the computer room where each girl sat at one of the three computer desks while I stood. I addressed the subject of tricks and gave them a quick rundown why rich men in general explored the underground sex world and mouse around with prostitutes.

"Well, one of the main reasons," I told them. "Is because they can't be themselves at home. An invitation to a private party on the other hand, has the tendency to hype them up to where they can create sects, cults and private clubs in their own twisted mind. It makes them feel like an insider, someone with connections and overall it gives them a reason to let their hair down. A lot of tricks, especially the rich and wealthy have perverted fetishes and obsessive fantasies that they must by all means, keep on the low because it could interfere with their normal conduct of life, or when put into practice it could get them a good ol sexual misconduct charge. Better yet, expose their mental illness." I told them. "The rich and wealthy people that you see every day appear sane on the exterior but are actually fucked up, psychotic and mentally deranged on the interior. Not all of them, but the ones who explored the underground sex world do not pose a physical threat because they are stimulated by knowing that you can welcome and hold water with their secrets. They seek the kind of taboo sex acts that they can engage in that tends to be depersonalized and ritualistic." I laced them up with paraphilia's, which is to describe the out of the ordinary sex practices. "Masochism for example, is the wish to suffer pain and humiliation. Exhibitionism, the need to expose their dicks in public. Transvestitism, the desire to dress up in girls' clothing. Voyeurism, gaining pleasure from watching others fuck. Amaurophilia, The appeal to have sex while blindfolded.   Coprophilous, sexual attraction to shit. Gerontophilia, the sexual attraction to their grand moms and pedophilia, the sexual attraction to their kids."

I addressed these subjects so when they see the shit; pun very much intended, then they wouldn't be shaken up. I don't care what these tricks do or how they do it, I'm not in the game to judge. I'm only in the game for one reason, and that's to reach deep down in their pockets, feel me? I do not however, advocate anything that has to do with children. However, I will play the shit outta them. Razzle-dazzle, outwit, benefit with interest from the rich trick does not disturb my conscience one bit.

While Carmen hopped on the computer, I worked with

Alisha on her speech and gave her a demonstration on how to work with Tabatha. They both have individual projects so it's almost mandatory that they know their rolls to play. Alisha absorbs information smoothly and is quick on the draw. She is not the type of bitch that you would have to beat upside the head over and over just so she could retain what's being exercised. Break it down to her one time and she's on top of it. I can hardly wait to see her in action Saturday.

I took off in the lac. First, I went to Beaumont and got fitted for a deluxe Armani tuxedo, which I was told would be ready first thing in the morning. Then I swung in a computer repair shop, where I was able to build with a young, brilliant Asian dude named Khan. After a twenty minute conversation with him, I hired him right there on the spot. I gave him my card, address and agreement that if he wanted to make a couple of stacks, then to show up at my crib tomorrow, two o'clock sharp. "No problem." Khan said as he caught on to the fact that I was about business. I stopped at an upscale furniture outlet and copped a 15-foot, blue Lacquered, Dakota Jackson dining room table and likewise, it will be delivered tomorrow. It's an enormous table with gigantic legs, so I know it's going to take at least professional movers and a large ass truck to get it to the house.

By the time I was back at the house, Urma was there with the whole get up; cleaning supplies, uniform on and the eagerness to get to work. She told me in Spanish that her daughter would be here to pick her up at six o'clock every day. But, she felt the need to remind me, "Except for

Sundays." I told her that I was thinking about hiring a cook for the party and as a result, off the top she felt disrespected. She told me in Spanish.

"If you are too good to eat my cooking, then there's no need for me to be here."

Right then I knew it was a false move so I tried to clean the shit up. "Oh mi senor Urma, I was only playing with you to see where you was at. I would be delighted to eat your cooking."

"Mm.hm." She responded with flat lips. I told her that we were having a Grande fiesta and she agreed to have everything ready by Saturday.

Friday was tight; it was the last day of the invitations and the first day to set up. Carmen said that there were now two hundred and twenty-four members to Threat To The World Entertainment. I told her to cut the invitations off because you don't have to be a calculus wiz to come to the realization that the numbers were in my favor. Just like my dude, Denzel said in Training Day, "I'm winning." And now it's pronounced clear as vodka "King Kong ain't got shit on me!"

I stepped on the gas and shot off to Beaumont to pick up my tuxedo. While I was still in Beaumont, I checked on Khan and he was psyched up for his project. Right away, he laid down the groundwork. I rented sixty folding chairs, ten folding tables, twenty-five 30-inch flat screens and ten tablets with credit card strips from his shop. He said that he would take care of the rest, including installment and delivery. He said that all bases were covered except that I needed to go to my bank and set up credit card decentralization to the Threat To The World business expansion account. "I'm on it." I told him, but I ran into an obstacle because this process took up majority of my damn day.

Time is money, I'm thinking while I was held hostage at the bank. Nonetheless, while I was there I went ahead and withdrew some money so I could give Urma, Khan and the seven girls that were expected to show up tomorrow at noon.

When I finally made it to the house, I rolled up behind Khan's white cargo van. He was already in motion. He brought the chairs, TV's, tablets, tables and there was loose wires every damn where. He was also red in his Chinese golden face because of all the half buck-naked girls flaunting around. Tabatha said.

"He's cute in all but goddamn, he's shy as hell. All he's done is stare at the ground while he's been hooking all this stuff up."

I told her that he wasn't here to kick it; he's busy so stay the fuck outta his way. I know that pussy can be a heavy distraction so I had to catch his back by running her ass off. Later that day he told me that he built a webpage for Threat To The World Entertainment. To Top it off, he installed a Sony surround sound system in the entire house and said that he could DJ the party from his laptop. This dude is multitalented, smart, hardworking, follows protocol and most of all; he's playing with a full deck.

I wanted him on the team but still I didn't want to come off too strong with the proposition to where it would give him the impression that my back was to the wall, or if I was hard up. I decided after the party that I would toss a few numbers at him that he couldn't refuse.

Before nightfall, the table finally showed up with four niggas complaining about the fact that they would have to disassemble the table to get it inside the house. I'm thinking; that's your muthafucking job ain't it? But check game; I compromised with them and told them that if they could air out everything in the first guest room to the right of the living room, set the table up in there and move swift, then they could have everything that was in there, including a c-note a piece. On the dot, they jumped on the offer and was wrapping everything up in an hour in a half tops. Free shit and a tip motivated my niggas to move quick.

The girls were knocked out, and right before my eyes came to a close, my phone lit up on vibrate with a text. I saved her name to my contacts the last time I missed her call so I wasn't surprised to see Shanna as the sender. I read it as it said: WELL?

I texted my address and told her to be here tomorrow at twelve o'clock sharp and to be prepared to cater to well over two hundred horny men.

CHAPTER 17
MASQUERADE

D-day, the day of the party was introduced with; "What's the plan Threat?" Carmen asked me while we were taking our last bites of sliced oranges and fried eggs we were eating for breakfast. After wiping my mouth with a paper towel, I said.

"The plan is to stay focused. Today if you are experiencing any fluttery feelings, like butterflies in your stomach, nausea or negative energy building up, then close your eyes and take in a calming breath. While your eyes are still closed, picture us at the top. The top of success while clinching tight to greatness, feel me?"

They all nodded their head but for some reason they seemed spaced out as if, they were in a complete daze. They were in a dream state, assuming from my end that they were replaying the event in their dome over and over again which was causing bullshit worrying, maybe even thinking about worst-case scenarios. But see, that's when the doctor in me kicked in because I knew the cure to bullshit fears and senseless phobias. I knew the best medicine, the proper and well-suited tranquilizer to sedate their nerves. I told Alisha to hurry up and grab a glove. When she came back, I fucked all three of them right there in the breakfast room. Tabatha called me the medicine man and at that moment, I knew that three doses of hard dick was the best pharmaceutical for the heebie-jeebies.

At 8:43 AM, I was pulling my shorts up and shaking my joint back to its resting place. Seconds later, Urma was at the door while the girls raced each other upstairs.

"Buenos Dias." Urma greeted me with a wide smile and in a polite manner. She came in with her daughter carrying several glass casserole pans with layers of foil wrapped over the top. It was precooked meat so the aroma seeping through the foil was smacking me directly in my face. Apparently, it was a Mexican cuisine, home cooked meal and no doubt, she took pride in her shit.

I ran to her daughter's car to get the rest of the warm pans and as soon as I stepped in the kitchen, I noticed Urma sniffing her nose and taking in quick whiffs as if she were trying to trace a particular odor like a hound dog. Off the top, I realized that Urma smelt the sex that was drifting in the air.

Urma told her daughter that she would see her at six o'clock.

I caught on quick, so I peeped that was her way of saying, "Adios, now be gone." I also noticed her daughter scoping me out from the corner of her eye while she was helping put the food up. Thick! That's the best word I could come up with to describe her daughter's short, compacted, coke bottle frame. Not fat, I said thick, which means she's hella fine. She stood at around 5'3 and looked to be more or less in the ballpark of twentyish. She had long, silky, dark hair traveling down to the center of her back.

She has perfectly pouty and luscious lips, nice D cup size titties and a gluteus maximus that made J Lo's ass look like pancakes. I thought to myself, little girl you best keep your eyes in check before you find yourself being pursued by a pimp.

As soon as she left, I jetted straight to the master shower. Carmen was in there and I could hear her soft voice behind the bathroom door singing along with the shower radio. I took my clothes off, I opened the medicine cabinet, put another condom on and fucked Carmen's brains out in the shower. I made damn sure that her screams were loud enough for Alisha and Tabatha to hear. This way I would be able to diagnose everyone's frame of mind.

When we stepped out of the shower would there be growls, pursed lips, rolled eyes and unnatural silence? Would I have to regress all the way back to the fundamentals just to explain to Alisha that this is part of the game? That this is 'Case In Point' what goes down within the lifestyle of a pimp? That in fact I didn't twist anyone's arm, put a gun to, or gorilla my way inside anyone's head? When we stepped in the bedroom all we heard was giggling and mimicking. Alisha did an impression of Carmen.

"Oh, oh Threat, oh my God, oh, oh my God. Damn bitch, sound like you caught the holy ghost in there." Alisha said with one hand above her head while turning around in circles with her eyes closed.

"Hallelujah, praise the lord, oohhh hallelujah."

Alisha and Tabatha cracked up laughing and automatically I knew without any doubt that today was going to be a good day.

At 10:32 AM, Khan was at the front door. He asked me to look outside at his van. When I pulled the curtains back, I seen that he had a large trailer attached to his van with two Escalade golf carts parked on it. I never seen an Escalade gulf cart and I got to admit that they were fly but I told him, "My dude, don't get it twisted, the carts are dope and all but what makes you think I need a golf cart? Do it look like I play golf?"

With a quick sarcastic come back, he said. "I don't know what a person is supposed to look like who plays golf but I know that you definitely need these carts."

I lost eye contact with Khan: I found myself staring straight ahead while at the same time beating up my brain. This little motherfucker is intelligent so I knew he had the ups on me. I felt wide open, slipping a matter fact because he knew something that I missed. Time is ticking, besides I was tired of doing guesswork so I threw in the towel. I took a small step back then I asked him.

"Why do I need them Khan?"

"Well yesterday on my way home I calculated the distance from the driveway to the main street, and the street is a half mile long. We're talking about two thousand, six hundred and forty feet. So I had a hunch that you intend to use the street for parking right? But there's only one problem."

"What's up?

"Rich people are not going to walk a half mile anywhere. I don't care how super-duper your girls look."

I was Impressed with his observation. I also knew what he was shooting at. Someone could escort the trick from their vehicles to the circle driveway in the gulf carts VIP style.

When leaving they could do the same process. But who? Who's going to chauffeur them on a round trip back and forth? surely, it's not him because he'll be mixing music, recording video, showing video, the whole nine. I know it's not me because I'm the live host. I know damn well it's not one of the girls because they'll be fucking. Was there a glitch in his grand idea, or did he have that figured out too? Right before I could ask him, he already beat me to the punch line.

"Two of my coworkers from the shop will be here at seven; I mean if that's cool with you. But I reassure you that they're level headed and I'm pretty sure you'll approve of them."

"Roger that!"

Absolutely I have a spot for him on the team. On the money, Khan is what I needed in order to take my vison to the next level. A team is a body of associates who have the same vision but peek through different binoculars. A team is strategically engineered into a moving force of, not one but a wide variety of skills, talents and the knowhow. What you think moves the body? Do you think a football team would be able to move down a field with eleven quarterbacks?

Alisha said that the three girls from Player's didn't need

a ride but three of the girls from Orange did. It wasn't a problem though because her Mexican home girl Maria had it covered. Alisha went to the pool area to set up chairs while Urma had the whole kitchen occupied. Khan attached the two Escalades to a charger and said that he would have to do a few particular details to the sound system, TV's and tablets. Carmen and Tabatha were setting up all the alcoholic beverages on a large folding table, catty-cornered to the left of the wet bar. Everyone was busy. Most of all, everyone knew their role to play.

At 11:36 AM Shanna was at the door. She was casually dressed in her laid-back demeanor with blue denims, a number 29 Seattle Seahawks jersey and solid white air force ones. She was hauling a large leather handbag on her shoulder. When I tried to offer my assistance for the bag, she said.

"No I'm good, I just need to know where to set up and if you have a large jar so I'll be able to collect tips?"

I smirked on the inside at her nonchalance, as if nothing else mattered apart from business. Which is cool. Still there's formalities, like; how are you doing? Are you having a good morning? She could have even said. "I like your house." Because I noticed her eyes gazing around as if she just found herself lost in the crib of Leonardo Da Vinci. That's when I snapped that the bitch was putting up a brick wall that she figured would be a solid defense mechanism. No big deal because I was amused by staring at this dazzling work of art. Her dark, chocolate almond skin is smooth and flawless so she didn't need makeup, and she wasn't wearing any other than lip-gloss, therefore placing her in a category in between divine and angelic. Her titties were mediocre but her ass made up for it tenfold. She was fine in every sense of the word, with just enough attitude to keep a nigga on his toes. She wore a short haircut, even shorter than Maya's but hers has an original style to it. A style only rocked by a bitch who is one thousand percent sure of her elegance and structure of her face. I had to laugh at myself sitting up here struggling to stay focused. Snapping back quick, I said.

"There won't be any cash transactions here tonight Shanna so a jar won't be needed."

She narrowed her slanted shaped eyes at me. "Then how will I draw in tips? I will cater the party for a flat rate but still Threat, tips are mandatory."

"No need to get your nerves all bent up outta shape." I said. "I will explain everything when the rest of the girls show up. In the meantime, relax and make yourself comfortable. If you want, you can go over there with the girls so you can get familiar with what you'll be serving to drink tonight."

She glanced over at Carmen and Tabatha by the wet bar. They were telling jokes, laughing out loud with fluid body movement. She turned back towards me then said.

"I'm good!"

I left her to it. She's fine, straight up, but I didn't have time to be pampering or even patronizing. When I bounced, she just stood there with her mouth open. I guess one way or another she'll come to the realization that I got shit to do. I slid the glass door open and went outside by the pool area with Alisha. She was setting the chairs up in six rows, parallel from each other. There are sixty chairs so there are ten rows going horizontal. If you didn't know what was actually jumping off here tonight, then you could easily mistake it for a small wedding reception. When I walked up to Alisha, she wasn't talkative so much like her regular self. She gave me the impression that she was trying to stay busy, maybe to keep other shit off her mind. I walked behind her with my hands in my pocket.

"What's up Alisha?"

"Hey."

"Are you good?" I asked her while she suddenly stopped moving the chairs around.

"Yeah, I'm straight. Why, what's up?"

"I don't know baby, I mean you just seem distant. But if there's something that you want to get off your mental, then we can build if you want to."

She smiled but I didn't ask her why because I already knew that the melody of the word 'Baby' rolling off my tongue in reference to her was music to her ears. It was personal and I also knew that this was the type of shit she likes to hear. She wants to feel special and secluded from the rest. When I ate her pussy the other day, I intended for her to see the brighter picture. That she is special. That she is my number one. That she is the alpha and the omega of this entire body. She looked up at me with her beautiful hazel brown eyes, and then said.

"No one, I mean no one in this world would ever be able to convince me to do what I'm doing tonight. Don't get me wrong, I don't have any regrets because trust, I'm already knowing we're going to be large. Besides, there's something about you that's so powerful and supreme. Seriously though, because don't you know that I still get a tingling sensation in my pussy when I get next to you?"

I laughed. "That's what's up Alisha." I said. "Without you then none of this would even be possible. You set the tone and the standard for any and every bitch that steps foot in my circle." I moved her curly hair from her face while she looked up at me.

The sun was fiercely blazing down on us but still, there was a gust of wind breezing through, causing it to lighten the burden from the scorching heat. Which called attention to this point in time: Take the negative with the positive, and then the positive will always outshine the negative.

I grabbed Alisha from the back of her head. I brought her closer to me with my fingers clinched tight to her hair. I kissed her but it wasn't a regular kiss. A magnetic attachment drew in power from the god's above. We were standing in front of the six rows of chairs as if this set up was destined exclusively for us.

"You may now kiss the bride." I heard a voice come from behind us. Little did I know, but we were on stage. When I separated my mouth from Alisha's, her mouth was still open but her eyes remained closed. When I turned around, it wasn't just one person; no sir, it was a whole audience of spectators now clapping in shit. I shot a quick glimpse at my watch and seen that it was five minutes after twelve. It wasn't until then that I noticed that everyone showed up at the same time.

"Now that's a good look." A tall black chick said. "Alisha, I ain't even gonna lie girl, y'all make a cute ass couple."

For the first time I saw Alisha blushing with a sparkle in her eye, which gave me the impression that she took the girl's statement as a compliment. Alisha looked at her with a grin.

"Thanks Moniqua, how long y'all been standing there?"

"For starters." The Mexican chick interrupted. "Long enough to get hot and bothered, I'll tell you that much. But damn Alisha, you said he was fine and yes indeed, he is. But I wasn't expecting the nigga from the soap operas."

They all cracked up laughing. Then another black chick said. "Oh shit, you sholl right; he do look like that nigga Shamar Moore."

Alisha fixed her eyes on the Mexican chick then said. "Maria shut the fuck up, don't start okay?"

"Oh believe me." Maria said. "I ain't even got warmed up yet."

Carmen made her way through the crowd of girls. She showcased three white girls to her right side. They all had determined stares with probing eye contact. No laughs, just tight grips to the straps on their backpacks. The one furthest to the right tossed her long red hair back then shook her head. That's when Carmen said.

"I have no idea how Alisha pulled this off, but these three bitches right here are no nonsense and like so dedicated to their talents. Muhammad is a total loser for not acknowledging their potentials. But really, kudos to Alisha for recruiting these girls because they're definitely five star quality."

I paid close attention to the three white girls. I noticed how they were watching the other four Orange girls to see their reactions to Carmen's endorsement. At the same time, I peeped how the four Orange girls increased their distance from the white girls with mumbling underneath their breath. Remember, when dealing with female emotions, hormones in such, shit can get dangerous. Throw a little animosity in the mix, and then the shit can get catastrophic. All at once, I felt the need to jump in the driver's seat before these hoes crash out.

"Alright, listen up everyone." I said. "We're about to build out here for a while, so if you don't mind, I'm gonna need you to catch a squat in one of these chairs."

Maria's head flinched back with a wrinkled up nose. While they walked to the chairs, she glanced around the pool area with a waving hand. In a skeptical tone, she said. "I know I'm Mexican in all, but sweetheart I don't do construction. What in the hell we gonna build?"

"A relationship." I said with a relaxed posture as I stood in front of the girls sitting in the chairs. "But see, if you could shut the fuck up, maybe for ten minutes then I can give you the run down."

"No he didn't." I heard Maria say under her breath. But still, she took heed to what I said because she now had a strap on her muzzle with her arms crossed. I heard the other girls giggling.

The tall chick who Alisha called Moniqua had her hand to her mouth while it was balled up into a fist. "Oooh, check that hoe mane!"

Seconds before I was about to press on, Alisha said.

"Hold up daddy."

She ran in the direction towards the house, she opened the glass slide door, then a minute in a half later she came back with Shanna. While she ushered Shanna to the chairs, I winked my eye at Alisha then got the ball rolling.

"Alright, now where was I?" I stared hard into Maria's eyes then said. "Like I said, we're going to build out here for a while. The standard English dictionary has four definitions for the word build. First it could mean your physical structure; you know, like as in what type of build you have. Second, it could mean to increase or accelerate as in, to build up. Third it could mean to construct, which Maria right here clearly knows everything about."

They all giggled while Maria sighed with exaggeration and she crossed her arms tighter to her large titties. I stepped to her where she was sitting on the first row, directly in front of me. I gave her a playful nudge to her shoulder to relax her nerves, then I continued.

"But we're going to ride out with the last one, and that's to establish, touch bases, where like I said...To build a relationship. And you know just as well as I know that the basic principles in kicking off any relationship is a proper introduction. To those of you who don't know; my name is Threat. I'm biracial, black and white; best of both worlds baby! I'm 32 years young. Born and raised in Minneapolis, Minnesota. Bounced back and forth from Dallas to my city for a couple of years. Did a 12 year bid, now I'm standing here in front of you. See how simple that was? Basically what I'm trying to say is that you can sum up your life story in a couple of sentences. So I figure that we can do this in a sequence, something like a chain reaction, feel me? So when I point to you, lace me up just like I laced you up."

I started on the first row to my right. I pointed at a short mahogany skin toned chick with zig-zag braids in a wicked ass design.

"Well Alisha said not to tell you any nick names but my name is Peaches; no lie, it's on my birth certificate and everything. I'm 22 and yes, I do have I.D. I'm full black, nothing blended. Born and raised here in the fruit. I got two kids and my baby daddy is on lock. Anything else?"

I smirked on the inside. On the real, I dig these Orange chicks. Even if they are 'messy'. Show me a bitch that ain't messy, that's just a female's nature. But it goes to show you that ain't no hood different from the next. Flavor and attitude is global.

"No Shorty, that was perfect. Just make sure you have that I.D handy because I'm gonna need to see that."

Still on the first row, I skipped Alisha which caused her to stick her tongue out at me. I paid her no attention then pointed at Maria who was face to face with me. Now Maria is an exotic beauty. She caught my eye the very first moment she stepped up in this bitch. Big titties like Carmen, standing at around 5'8. Shirley Temple curls, pretty brown eyes with a righteous ass. She could easily pass for a younger version of Eva Mendez. But still I had to bring her down a little bit to that level I like to call reality.

"Can I talk now?" Maria asked me but I didn't give her any feedback, I just pierced my eyes into hers until she caught on to the fact that I didn't have time to entertain any bitch ass games.

"Okay, okay, look I think we're starting this relationship off on a bad note. Maria said. "I'm actually a cool ass person, you can even ask Alisha. Me and that bitch went to school together so she knows what's up. Matter of fact I always been the damn fool and class clown so you gonna have to expect me to say some off the wall shit. Like you remember Alisha when I...

Right away, Alisha cut her off. "Get to the point bitch, we don't have time to be reminiscing in shit."

"Okay already! Damn, you muthafuckers up in here is mean. Anyway, my name is Maria Velazquez. I'm 21 with no kids. I was raised here in Orange but my whole family is from Guadalajara, Mexico. The first motherfucker call me a wet back, we fighting."

Everyone laughed and while Maria was twirling her Shirley Temple curls with her finger, she glanced up at the sky then said, "Let's see; um, what else? Oh yeah, in my spare time I like to fuck, suck and swallow so if you have any openings then I would make a perfect candidate. I already done told Alisha that I want to do what she's doing. I have my own transportation, no baby daddy drama, I have..

I quickly cut her off. "Do you have I.D?" When she said. "Sure do." I pressed on to the next one. No one was sitting on the second row except Shanna. I skipped her then went straight to the third row. I directed my attention to the first chair to my left was sitting a tall, cherry brown complected chick with flawless skin like a Cover Girl, except there was no photo shop here; it was all natural. She was blessed with a dope figure so I would like to think of her as 'Banging And Sassy'. I nodded my head to her then asked her.

"Your name is Moniqua, right?"

"Already!" She said. "I'm that bitch Moniqua. I'm from the fruit but I don't be fucking with these nigga's around here like talking bout. The one's who be balling on a budget? Ain't nothing worse than a broke ass nigga. Anyway, I be getting it in. I play the field at the casino, Delta Downs in Louisiana. You can catch me on Name your Price.com, Backpage, Tagged and I got regulars too. So I'm experienced, if you get my drift? I'm 25, I'm black but they say I'm for a Dominican nigga. I don't know the loser so who know's. And FYI, I can provide I.D."

"Perfect." I said. Then I shot my attention to the girl sitting right next to her. She's light skin, almost the same complexion as Alisha except this girl has a little orange mingling with the yellow. Her hair is styled in an artful conception with blond highlights swirling across her forehead. She looked shy, almost timid but all in all, she was drop dead gorgeous. I noticed her gripping tight to her purse that was sitting in her lap. She was looking down at first, but I guess she suddenly became aware of the fact that she was about to be called on because she slowly looked up at me and cleared her throat.

"Hey. She said. Then looked around before she continued in a soft and sexy accent. "Ma name is Chasity. Um from Baton Rouge, Louisiana. Um creole. Um 20 and.. I goh to Lamar."

"That's it?" I asked her. Then she snapped with

unexpected life resurrecting in her eyes.

"Oh yah, I gat ma driver's license end school I.D."

I left her alone and thought to myself: Maybe she was like Janet Jackson. She's shy when she's in her natural element but a fucking beast on the stage and a complete freak in the sheets. I know her kind. Besides, if she knows Alisha then she has to have something pornographic going on.

I bounced over Carmen and Tabatha who were sitting on the middle row, then I went straight to the three white girls who were sitting far in the back on the last row of chairs. Which by the way, was ironic as fuck to me. I didn't think twice of it though because I was pressing for time. Therefore, I knew I had to fast forward this introduction because there was a lot more to cover. I was sizing the three white girls up as I took notice to their strong posture, yet they had a sense of calm and ease. They knew that they were beyond any shadow of doubt, 'Top Notch' and it was spelled out clear that they could care less what the others thought.

The redhead chick has big freckles but she didn't remind me of Pippy Longstoking. More like she could be the very picture of a physical fitness model. Her toned and defined legs, flat and bricked up stomach, firm and round ass was all advertised tight and right in her white Adidas skin tight fitted spandex suit. The other two white chicks sitting next to her was pretty much equipped with the same shit, except one was blond with red highlights and the other one had jet black hair with bedroom eyes like Mila Kunis. I paid attention to all three of them then said. "From a mile away I can clearly see that you three work together. So this is how it's gonna go down. I want one of you, I don't care who it is; I want you to represent for all three of you. Let me hear what you got."

As I figured, the tall redhead stood up without needing a stamp of approval from the others. I identified her as the mistress a long time ago. Spotting the head is a nuts and bolts strategy that you should by all means tighten up in all aspects of life. Even if a crew of ants were to mob in your crib, there's still a queen ant somewhere in the mix. Without the head, the rest will crumble.

"Hi, my name is Heather and I'm 24 years of age." She said, sounding like a commercial advertisement. "This magnificent blond next to me, her name is Dakota and she's also 24. The gorgeous one next to her; well that's Abby and she's 22. We are originally from Great Falls, Montana to the east of the Rocky Mountains. Anyhow, Alisha knows that we are here only for a short period of time because at Player's we could not reach an agreement with the manager. We are independent but we have worked with several agencies across the U.S, as well as the U.K, Tokyo and Brazil. Alisha says that your agency is the best that Texas has to offer so we decided to give it a shot. Added to the fact that Alisha is so awesome so we trust her judgment. And yes, you are dead on because for sure we work together as a 'Three Girl Show'. We can offer a hot voyeur demonstration and we also welcome all fetishes including dominatrixrmx. If you would like to refer your clientele to our credentials, then they can view our website at www.Globalthreegirlshow.com. Yes of course we can definitely provide identification, visa and passports. Thank you so much for the opportunity."

All the girls were now turnt around in their seats staring at the three white girls as if now all of a sudden they were marveled by their professionalism. A threefold powerhouse who saw only green through their binoculars. Now that's my kind of language.

But check game, after the introduction I became conscious to the fact that they just raised the bar to everyone's pay day. The Orange girls should be thanking them right now. I formed my hands in the image of a box and signaled for Alisha to go get one. While she took off, I said.

"Alright, thanks everyone. For any of you who do not know Carmen, well that's the blond in the middle row and sitting next to her is Tabatha."

They both raised their hand up and started twisting it side to side as if they were contestants in a beauty pageant.

"Sitting on the second row by herself; that's Shanna and she will be our wonderful waitress for the night."

Shanna didn't raise her hand or even acknowledge herself. She just continued to dig in her large bag as if she was looking for something lost. It didn't matter though because right on cue, Alisha was walking through the entrance with the box in her hands. She closed the glass slide door with her heel from her foot, then I said.

"And Alisha here needs no introduction."

They all giggled while I glanced at my watch and seen that it was five minutes to one, I said.

"But in seven hours from now some of you will be

introduced to a life that's foreign to you. You might even run across a few things that you don't necessarily agree with. But just like a sewage worker, he may or may not get a kick out of indulging with shit, but he tolerates it because he knows at the end of the day he's getting paid. With that said, I will pay each of you five thousand dollars for your talents tonight."

"Five thousand dollars?" Peaches said. "Shid, I was expecting a couple of big faces or something. But five racks? Now you got my attention pimpin."

"He's had my attention a long time ago." Maria said, while the rest of the Orange girls had wide smiles, glancing around to see if the others were experiencing the same thing. But the 'Three Girl Show' girls weren't smiling. They only had blank stares as if five thousand dollars wasn't shit to them but a measly pair of Gucci shoes. On the other hand, their representative was now standing, so I said. "What's up Heather?"

"We would like to know your tipping system and what percentage is divided?"

She asked me. But see, I know that any bitch or anybody for that matter who's involved in the pussy selling business knows that flat rates ain't shit. A flat rate is nothing but a talking fee or just for a hoe to show up at your door, or to open hers. The real money is involved with tips. A real talented bitch who knows how to execute her powers will have a trick tipping on the grounds of removing her shoes. It's called the fine print! The clause that comes with strings attached, but the trick has no other choice but to toe in line because his dick has overpowered his common sense. But dig, I was expecting this as to why I upped the flat rate.

"How does five thousand dollars accommodated with 50 percent tips sound?"

Heather glanced down at Dakota and Abby. They were shaking their head up and down in agreement. Heather shook her head up and down in agreement. Then she looked at me and shook her head up and down in agreement. Everything was agreed. I nodded my head at Alisha then said.

"Alisha is going to hand you a white domino mask. It covers only half of your upper face where it fits appropriately on the ridge of your nose like glasses. Everyone here tonight will have one on, including our guest."

Alisha put the mask in circulation while Maria's crazy ass put the mask on, then pulled her hair back over the elastic string. She was dancing and bouncing in her chair as if she was grooving to a salsa beat. Her arms were in motion and her lips were puckered out. But I didn't give her the attention she was seeking because my eyes were on the rotation of the mask. As soon as Abby took possession of the last mask, I said.

"Besides heels, makeup and perfume, the mask is the only thing you'll be wearing tonight does anyone have a problem with that?"

"I sure in the hell don't" Moniqua said. "I like the way you think. And besides, I'm very confident with this body."

"I don't have a problem with it either papi." Maria said. "Once you see all of this then maybe you'll get your heart right."

Alisha opened her mouth to say something to Maria but I cut her off. "Alright, no protest on the wardrobe obligations; that's what's up! Girls, I want you to know that tonight this house is going to be packed to its fullest capacity. The gentlemen you see here will have only one or two statuses and that's either rich or wealthy. When we post or advertise we use the term 'Upscale Gentlemen', so they respond because they get the idea that we actually mean 'Rich Muthafuckers Only.' But see, there's a certain protocol that must be followed when dealing with muthafuckers who are made of money. If you are unfamiliar with what I'm stressing, then I want you to pick a girl and build with her until you click to what needs to be done. I prefer you to pick either Carmen, Alisha, Heather, Dakota or Abby. Moniqua, I know you're experienced but we're talking about an entirely different class of ballers so I'm gonna need you to build with someone other than that, are there any questions?"

Alisha said. "Daddy, this ain't a protest, it's only a question alright?"

"What's up Alisha?"

"Well, I like the idea of being naked with only heels and these mask; that's sounds sexy as hell. But I think we would look something like erotic if we had on thigh highs. I think we could work it, I mean that's just my opinion."

I looked at the rest of the girls. "How many of you feel the same way?"

It was a unanimous decision. Everyone simultaneously raised their hand up, including Shanna so I granted Alisha's petition.

"Thigh highs it is, but nothing else. Next you'll be asking me if you can wear a goddamn robe."

They all laughed then I brought the meeting to a close.

"Tonight there will be plenty of alcohol. I want you to limit yourself to one glass, that's it. And, the only reason I'm even suggesting that is so you can loosen up a little bit. But don't get full or anything close to tipsy because I don't have time to be catering to a house full of drunk bitches, feel me?"

They giggled then I said. "Alright, let me leave you with this then I'm gonna fall back." I cleared my throat then said. "Erase the word fun from your mental, and replace it with work because getting paid is essential. We ain't here to have a blast, our only mission is to make that cash, so in the mean-time please 'Splash' some water on that ass and don't act like a rookie. Because overall a nigga don't have time to be advertising any funky ass pussy."

They all cracked up laughing, and as I stood there watching them slap their knees, falling against each other's shoulder and wiping their tears, I suddenly felt like I was in a trance state. Their laughs became silent as if either I went deaf or everyone all at once went mute. But I wasn't tripping though, because as they seemed to be moving in slow motion, my mind was traveling like the speed of light. As a pimp, I put my foot in the door and at this moment the world is a stage and I'm the headliner in it.

"Threat!" Alisha said interrupting my thoughts. When

I said "What's up Alisha?" You could almost hear the tires skidding on everyone's laughs. They stared at me as if I just lost my damn mind. That's when I realized that it wasn't Alisha's voice I heard; it was the one inside my dome. On the spur of the moment, the scene became awkward. All you could hear at this point was the water in the pool rippling from the wind. But I thought on my toes because as I walked towards the house, I played it off. "I said that's what's up Alisha! That's the spirit I need everyone to stay in for the remainder of the day."

I found solitude in the computer room and at 6:04 PM. I was walking Urma to the door. Once again she done her magic. She prepared chicken tacos, wrapped with corn tortillas. She used boneless and skinless chicken thighs with chopped onion, garlic cloves, avocado plum tomatoes and sour cream. She also had several large bowls of pork tenderloin salad displayed on three folding tables outside by the pool area. On the up and up, she had the whole enchilada, and I ain't talking about a figure of speech. There were rows upon rows of enchiladas on a separate table with chips, dips, fruit, rolls of deli varieties, salsa and peanuts. She provided all the necessary utensils, from plastic forks, paper plates and towels to Styrofoam cups. She even supplied heated inserts to keep the food warm. I'm convinced that Urma done this shit before or she has an extremely large ass family.

My dude Khan did his thizle too because there were flat screens everywhere. Outside by the pool area, in the dining room, living room, every guest room, master bedroom; he even had a few posted in the hallways. I'm glad he's finished because his so called sound checks was fucking with my nerves.

Shanna found something useful to do. She put throw pillows all throughout the house. She also put together a pallet made from pillows in front of the sixty chairs. She didn't surprise me though when I noticed that she rearranged the alcohol setup to her liking. The champagnes were now center front with the hard liquors in the back. There was another table with champagne glasses, shot glasses and several bowls of peanuts. My guess, the peanuts was Shanna's grand scheme to dehydrate them so they'll get familiar with saying 'Keep Em Coming.'

After building with the Orange girls, Carmen and Tabatha put together two hundred and twenty four party bags. Each bag contains the white mask and a variety pack of sexcessories. There's condoms, a six ounce bottle of K.Y lubricant jelly, a vibrator, handcuffs, wipes and a purple raffle ticket with a number in the center of the ticket.

After hopping out of the shower, putting on my tuxedo, throwing on my leather Gucci square toe shoes and spraying two shots of Gentlemen's Only Givenchy Intense cologne, I was feeling fresh to death. Khan was on point too in his tuxedo except he had his hair gelled into a Mohawk and his pants were skinny jean tight. He's 21 years young so I guess this is the leading edge fashion. The new generation of what young muthafuckers considered swag.

At 7:10 PM his two coworkers showed up wearing white crisp button down shirts, black silk vest with the same tight ass pants on. I just shook my head. One of the lil niggas was black and the other one was Mexican, so this tight pants wearing epidemic didn't appear to be any particular ethnic group. From what I'm seeing, it went viral. But you won't never see a pimp wearing tight ass pants though, I can guarantee you that much. A matter fact, I take that shit back. This is 2015!

I advised them to post up outside because rich people are never late. I told them not to be surprised if everyone showed up at the same time. I put a bug in their ear and told them to separate. One should position the Escalade gulf cart at the beginning of the street and the other one should be closer to the house, therefore they could work towards the middle in one accord. They wanted to convince me that they already had this planned. That's what's up!

It was fifteen minutes before eight when the girls came parading down the staircase in a single file line with Alisha in the front. They were all advertising their birthday suits with a mean strut, head high and their right hand was resting on their hips with their elbow extended into a 90 degree angle. They were all looking extraordinary with the white mask and enticing in their nakedness while making it known that they didn't have anything to hide because their curves, beautifully trimmed pussies, upright titties and glistening skin were all cheerfully exposed.

But something else in particular caught my attention. I recognized that they all had on the same shit. Same clear, see through six-inch stilettos. Same white fishnet, close fitted thigh high stockings with lace at the top. And I ain't even gonna ask where they got the same white gloves from because it wasn't in the wardrobe contract. On the inside I was aroused on an animated level, but still keeping it solid and nailed tight. I only asked.

"Who's idea was it to wear the same shit?"

Positioned in the middle of the staircase and standing in between Maria and Chasity; Carmen said.

"Of course it was Alisha's vision, but she almost freaked out because she was like, where in the hell are we going to find eleven pair of the same stockings? But it all worked out awesome because the 'Three Girl Show' girls miraculously had four pair of stockings each in their backpacks and these cute white leather gloves."

"Yeah." Alisha said. "And you already know every stripper is gonna have at least three or four pair of clear stilettos; it's a necessity."

She giggled. "And Maria supplied the Bare Mineral makeup products, Clinique vibrant red lipstick that you see on our lips and the Halle Berry Wild Essence perfume that you smell on our bodies. She has a few screws loose but the bitch was actually good for something."

I peeped how Alisha was trying to vouch for Maria. They were schoolmates no doubt, but Maria was also her alter ego. They stuck together, fought together, maybe even fucked the same niggas together. All in all, Alisha found an outlet from this miserable city and Maria wanted to roll no matter what the obligations were that came with it.

"You hear that papi?" Maria said. "See, I am good for something. You ain't know I was a makeup artist huh? I got a few other skills up my sleeve too."

I heard Maria loud and clear but my eyes were locked in on Shanna who was standing at the top of the staircase. She threw me for a loop because I wasn't expecting her to follow suit with the wardrobe demands. But there was no beef; she got in where she fit in and just like the other girls, she was straight up naked. Her Foxy Brown and ebony delight skin looked like melting chocolate, and right before my eyes, her kinky pussy hairs was skillfully carved into a diamond. Shanna looked like an exotic black panther with a white mask on, but I knew I had to stay focused because time was running out and ShowTime was approaching.

"Alright everyone, you look A1 superior. Straight up, you look so damn good that it clearly shows every sign of divinity. And that's how I want you to think, moreover 'Know' that you have the vigorous energy over these tricks tonight. Let these muthafuckers know that nothing in life comes without a price tag, And even if they already paid, it still comes with a burden that they're no stranger to; the sales tax..."

Right in the middle of my speech, little Peaches with the zig zag braids said, "Say Threat, you the shit pimp no lie!"

She threw me off guard but still it wasn't ill suited for this spotlight because I knew that this was the life they never experienced before. On the cool, neither have I but I envisioned it. And I know that once you form a mental picture of anything you can attract it with positive energy.

"No Peaches, you the shit shorty!" I said. "Everyone here is the shit. Now let's go to work. Alisha get in position and wait on my cue. Tabatha I need you on point baby girl."

Tabatha pointed two fingers to her eyes then pointed the same two fingers at me, then she nodded her head with a gangster ass look in her eyes. I continued.

"The 'Three Girl Show', you three already know your stage and Carmen, I need you in the foyer. Everyone else, pay attention, keep a smile on your face and let's get paid."

At 7:59 PM I walked Carmen to the foyer. There was a large amount of bags lined up in three rows and a tablet resting on top of the table that was now stationed next to the Chippendale stand. There was a dim light glowing from the light fixtures above our head which gave the area a calm and relaxed vibe.

At 8:00 PM on the dot, the doorbell rang. Before Carmen opened the door, she shook her hands then closed her eyes and took in a calming breath. I was putting the white mask on my face and she was opening the door at the same time.

"Welcome to Threat To The World Entertainment." Carmen said with a wide smile as she opened the door and greeted the guest with her naked body. A middle aged white man came through the door. He was a pleasant looking gent with salt and pepper hair that was seriously thinning at the top. But he looked like he had a vast reservoir of money so he could care less because his riches didn't show any sign of thinning. He was dressed in a black tailor made tuxedo, white cotton shirt, black silk tie and shiny black patent leather kicks. I noticed his gold cuff links had the initials D.T. That's when he said.

"Thanks for the invitation but Alisha Farrell is here, correct?"

"That is correct sir." Carmen said. "And believe it or not she has a surprise for you. Anyhow sweetie, I'm going to need your name so I can mark you off our guest list."

"Yes of course, my name is David Thornburgh."

Carmen scrolled down for David's name on the tablet. When she found it, she clicked on it by touching it with her finger. When his name highlighted, she said.

"Okay, here you are, David Thornburgh, guest number twenty three."

I found the bag with the number 23 written on it and gave it to Carmen. She gave the bag to David while she said.

"Inside this bag you'll find a white mask that is identical to the one this sexy gentleman and I are wearing right now. Please wear it and it would be in your best interest not to lose the ticket because you'll need it later."

She shook David's hand and stared at him with her enticing blue eyes, she said. "Awesome David. Thank you for becoming a member to Threat To The World Entertainment. Now you are on your way to a life of adult fun and pleasure."

As soon as David entered the house he was greeted with a thumping beat from Pitbull and the dude from Empire.

"All we want is a party, Have some shots with somebody, Take the music and turn it all the way up, If you came here to party, Ain't no doubt about it,
Ain't no no no no doubt about it..."

The beat continued thumping and the doorbell continued ringing. I didn't notice right off the top but it didn't take long for me to peep that a lot of them were being chauffeured to the masquerade in large, luxurious limousines. Which made it convenient for the valet parkers. All they had to do was instruct the chauffeur to come pick their parties up when they were notified.

By the time thirty minutes passed, the house was elbow to elbow deep with rich muthafuckers with lust and fascination in their eyes. I wasn't expecting it, but I didn't disapprove of it either when I seen that some of the guest brought their wives. You could hear loud conversations in several group settings and they didn't mind talking over the music. I was proud to see the Orange girls socializing on a large scale. They were cracking up with outburst of laughter while exchanging knowing looks with each other. Looks that said.

"I know these corny ass jokes ain't funny but just laugh anyway."

Every flat screen in the house was lit up with pornographic flicks. Each TV exhibited something different. Everything from Triple X hardcore, to soft porn, to dominaxtrix. Some even got a kick out of watching midget porn. Where Khan got this material? I have the slightest clue. But what I did know is that from a visual estimation, there had to be well over two hundred bodies up in here.

I scanned the whole house until I seen Tabatha sitting on a little white man's lap by the wet bar. She was playing with his hair while she had a slight pout in her bottom lip, giving her that adolescent, preteen disguise that she's been developing over the past week. I made my way to the foyer then stepped to Carmen.

"What we looking like?" I asked her while I glanced at

my watch. It was ten minutes after nine so I wanted to increase momentum by getting things rolling.

"Well, we're at two hundred and twenty three guest, not including the wives that some of these guys brought with them. But we're literally like waiting on one guest You know who!"

"If he don't show up within the next ten minutes, then we're gonna get this shit moving without him."

I examined the tablet then asked Carmen. "What number is Sean Nutter on the guest list?"

"He's number sixty six, but Alisha and Tabatha already came over here and hit me up for that information."

I pointed in the direction of the wet bar. "Is that him, the little motherfucker with Tabatha sitting on his lap?"

Carmen glanced over there with her neck stretched and she was standing on her tiptoes in her stilettos. She looked at me then said, "Yup, sure is."

My hoes are on point and from the looks of it, two steps ahead of me too. Hey, but I'm cool with that because at this point in the game, that's where I needed them; on top of everything! Plus it showed once and for all that my training paid off. Proper preparation prevents poor performance and any real pimp knows that your hoes presentation is the representation of your pimping.

On the other hand, after scanning the tablet I figured out who was missing. And right before I could cancel him out of the equation, Muhammad was making an entrance. Carmen politely gave him a bag, highlighted his name on the guest list, which was guest number one. He had an intense focus but with a cocky grin. He looked as if he were mentally fixating on his recent success. He asked me.

"Alisha, she's here right?"

I nodded my head one solid time, then he said. "Let's be honest, numero uno is a bit overpriced but I've got an adventurous soul, and my narcissism is balanced with a generous heart."

"Anything you say Muhammad." I said as I sympathetically patted him on his back while we approached the party. Bring your trick ass on, I thought; it's time to capitalize.

I stood in the middle of the largest area, which was underneath the archway that divided the living room and the dining room. I raised my hand for silence but with a playful grin to show comfort in the close proximity of all the guest. Within thirty seconds, the volume to the music died down and the conversations did the same. In addition, the pornographic flicks were no longer on the screens. I was now staring at my own image. I almost shook down every square inch of the house with my eyes in search of a camera but I kept it cool and solid like an iceberg. I only thought; Khan is a fucking beast!

"Alright, listen up everyone." I called out. "We're about to get everything underway. But before we do, I would like to give you a quote by Jay Z: 'You could be anywhere in the world right now, but instead you are here with us, and I appreciate that!'" They all chuckled, then I continued. "And to show my appreciation, I will relish in giving my word that before you leave here tonight you will experience complete satisfaction, you will be gratified, entertained and most of all, we will fulfill the bill.

Presented to you tonight is Threat To The World Entertainment, and without further ado...I do the honors of introducing Alisha Farrell."

Everyone in the house clapped, even the wives. There was a round of applause coming from a large audience by the pool area because they now had their eyes set on the screens that were installed outside. Then the screens went blank. Someone must have hit the switch to the lights too because it was now pitch black. The only source of light at this point were the screen savers that was now lit up from a handful of cell phones. Then out of nowhere, a loud roaring vibration erupted through the surround sound system. The kind of sound similar to what you hear at a cinema moments before the movie is featured. The words Threat To The World Entertainment was now smoothly gliding across the screens in a slideshow. Then an image of clear stilettos was shown on a concrete floor. I could tell it was the garage from the door in the background but there was no vehicle parked inside, only additional lighting and a stool that was positioned in the middle of the floor.

Click. Clack... Click.. Clack. The stilettos slowly progressed towards the stool. The sharp sound of the stilettos striking against the concrete floor echoed throughout the whole house. Then the camera slowly moved up the sunny colored legs with white fishnet stockings. The camera stopped at midpoint, enabling everyone to see the perfectly trimmed pussy hairs. The guest were turned on by the pussy shot because I could hear sounds of air sucking through their teeth and I noticed a few men giving a toast and there was even whistling.

The camera slowly climbed up her body while cruising pass her navel, pass her firm abdominal muscles, all at once showcasing them rocklike nipples. The circles around her nipples are the size of quarters but her nipples were on swollen so that's all you noticed. This was no doubt, the raw and uncut version of show and tell.

The camera zoomed out so you could now see Alisha's full view of her body while she was sitting in the chair. At first Alisha's legs were crossed but then she did one of them Sharon Stone, "Basic Instinct" moves. She uncrossed her right leg while flashing the inside of her pink pussy lips, then she politely crossed her left leg over her right leg. In a slow, mellow coaxing tone, Alisha spoke through every screen in the entire house.

"You like that don't you? Mmmm, well I like it more than you could ever imagine. Just the thought of pleasing you makes me horny. I want to fulfill your wildest desires and I want to know all your dirty little secrets. Your secrets are safe here because I know in the case of strippers, prostitutes and porn stars, you just love the sense of control with very little strings attached, don't' you? You know what else I know? I know that forbidden sex is something that gets rooted into your brain at an early age. From the time you had your naughty magazines hidden under your mattress to now where you cleared your internet browser history. You understand that society looks down at you for having a fling or for being entertained with sex acts if it's only for sport. Well shame on them! Who said you can't bust a nut and have your cake and eat it too?"

Everyone was laughing and clapping all at the same

time, while Shanna was making her rounds. Carmen came close to me with a bag in her hand while all the other girls lined up on the staircase. Everyone's laughs suddenly switched gears. They were now glancing around trying to put together what the fuck was up with all the unexpected movement. But it was obvious that Alisha could somehow see out here because as soon as everyone was in position, she said.

"Don't worry ladies and gentlemen, we're about to play a game. This is what I want you to do. I want you to reach in your bag and notice you'll find a cute little purple ticket. Also notice it has a number directly in the middle of it. What's this for? Well, we're about to do a raffle. We're going to draw a ticket from the bag that you see the wonderful blond, Carmen Styles holding."

Carmen held the bag up above her head and twirled around with an oversized smile on her face. As soon as she held the bag down, Alisha continued.

"In the bag there's two hundred and twenty-four tickets with your number on one of them. Who's ever number is drawed, then you'll win any girl you see lined up on the staircase. You'll get to take her upstairs to the master suite and have her alllll to yourself for the remainder of the night. If you want to share her then that's entirely up to you. But one of those sexy girls up there on that staircase is a virgin, so... Like I said, that's up to you."

They were now breaking their necks trying to see if they could spot the untouched girl. I seen a couple of them pointing and whispering amongst themselves as if they singled her out. Carmen shook the bag to win back everyone's attention. I could tell they were excited because I noticed a couple of them wetting their lips and some of the women were covering their face and peeking, but the drawing process was done quick and smooth. I pulled the ticket, gave it to Carmen, then she yelled out the number.

"Number sixty-six is the lucky number."

Alisha confirmed it through the screens. "Number sixty-six, you are the winner so you get to choose any one of the sexy girls, including me or Carmen Styles if you want."

"I'm sixty six, I'm sixty six, I'm sixty six." Sean Nutter blurted out while he gave Carmen his winning ticket. He's a small, frail dude who looked weak and scared of his own shadow. He wore a white tuxedo with a white bowtie with his white mask made him look like a white spot amongst all the black tuxedos. He walked over to the staircase, first passing the 'Three Girl Show' girls. He passed Maria without even looking her way. He passed Chasity, Moniqua, Peaches, finally he stopped at the top of the staircase directly in front of Tabatha, he said.

"I would love to have you for the night Tabatha."

Tabatha didn't say anything, she just bit her bottom lip, dropped her chin to her neck and in a slow unhurried paste, she escorted Sean to the master suite. Alisha on the other hand quickly spoke through the screens.

"Do you feel like he won and you lost? Well there's no losers here at Threat To The World Entertainment. Just your presence alone proves that you are the select members, not only to this bad ass sex club but to the whole world abroad. You are the upper class and the main choice who everyone wants to be. So you are the winners, you hear me? Tonight I want to guarantee your pleasure by making sure you find what you're looking for. I know that guys are pretty much on the same page when it comes to their ideal girl, be it for fantasy or reality. This is the part where we come in because I'm positive you'll find your type and what's sexy to you right here in this secluded house of exotic bitches. A place where you are free to be yourself and let your inhibitions go just like the wind. So enjoy the fruits of our labor, and keep in mind that these bitches are fucking, sucking and performing whatever kinky sexual acts that you can think of just for you. Let them know that they are appreciated, and that's enough to keep them sucking in their waist, spreading them legs, sticking out them titties and arching their back so that ass is just at the right angle to stimulate your thoughts of erotic entry. Now, tips are definitely accepted but not expected, but if you would like to tip any of the girls then we made it convenient for you."

Carmen held up one of several tablets so everyone could see.

Then Alisha said, "You can use one of the tablets like the one you see the wonderful Carmen Styles displaying. All you have to do is search for the girl's name by scrolling down with your finger, click on her name with your finger, and enter how much you would like to tip her with your finger. But the last part, you'll need to use your credit card by sliding it across the strip you see on the side of each tablet. Easy as 1, 2, 3."

Carmen slid an imaginary credit card across the strip

on the side of the tablet so our guest could see an example of how easy the process would be; while the whole time having a bright kool aid smile on her face. She looked like Racheal from The Price Is Right no doubt. Only this was the x rated version.

"Now with that said, I would like to ask everyone one simple question." Alisha asked everyone through the screens. "How many of you came here to see me?"

Everyone in the damn house bursted out in cheers, roars, barks and whistles, which lasted for a good 45 seconds. The camera zoomed in on Alisha's face with her white mask on. She covered her mouth with her hand and when she released it, she said.

"Wow, I'm so flattered. You guys make me feel like a celebrity or something. Okay, since you made me feel so amazing, I'm going to make you feel amazing too. Are you ready?"

More clapping came from the gentlemen but their claps were overwhelmed from the surround sound. Lady Gaga and R. Kelly was blasting through the speakers while more pornographic flicks popped up on the screens. All you could hear now was the loud beat and Lady Gaga's voice.

"Do what you want with my body, Do what you want, what you want with my body yeah."

Everyone's eyes lit up when they saw Alisha walking from the kitchen into the dining room, then entered the first guest room to the right of the living room. She sat her ass on the large 15 foot, blue lacquered, Dakota Jackson table. She scooted back until she was precisely in the middle of the table. She laid back, she stared at the light beaming from the ceiling and opened her legs spread eagle, then said.

"Who's going to fuck me first?"

I was now at the door with one of the tablets in my hand. I said, "Guest number one is Hussan Muhammad."

Muhammad entered the room with spark and gleam in his eyes. He gawked his eyes over Alisha's body while verbalizing his bullshit thoughts and feelings without hesitating. While unzipping his pants and loosening his belt, he said, "I've been waiting for this moment for a long time Alisha."

"Well then what are you waiting on?" Alisha said. "Fuck me Muhammad"

Muhammad took Alisha's advice and a whole ten minutes later he was walking out of the room tucking his shirt back into his pants. Guest number two, three, four and five came in at the same time and Alisha handled every guest like a pro. Men were now lined up in a line while leaning in trying to get a peek inside the room.

The'Three Girl Show' girls performed a voyeur show for sixty rubberneck peeping toms. They finally caught onto the fact that if they slid their cards then they could come up and join. Men were sliding their cards back to back on a wide scale. A couple of Houston based record producers didn't mind sliding their card for Maria who she had occupied with her mouth and a lot of other weird shit. They were in the furthest guest room down the hall, but to get there you had to maneuver through a lot of goddamn bodies because Peaches and Moniqua was doing the damn fool. The music was loud but you could still hear wet bodies slapping against their asses. They were side by side each other while men were lined up as if they were waiting on a bathroom stall.

Carmen entertained the guest wives' in a freaky fashion. She ate the wives' pussy while the husband fucked her from behind. Likewise, they didn't mind sliding their card as if it were a family extracurricular activity. Shanna was making her rounds and the guest most definitely became familiar with saying, "keep em coming".

I used the sixty seat stage by the pool area for something special. After the 'Three Girl Show' girls were wrapping up their show, I gathered up sixty of the most affluent muthafuckers that I could find. I stood Chasity in front of them and laced them up on a little secret. I dropped my voice to a whisper, as if anyone else in the world were listening. I said.

"She's the virgin!

Sean Nutter fell for the bait like I knew he would, considering Tabatha told him that she was only 14 years old. His twisted pedophile mind couldn't see past her revised age. He no longer desired Alisha because his lust was for a child. Which is why he didn't put up any kind of dispute paying the ten thousand dollar tax price. Yeah, we did a drawing but his ticket number 'Sixty-six' was gonna get called no matter what muthafucking number was drawed.

Muhammad likewise didn't buck against paying the ten thousand dollar premium it was going to take to lead the train. Ever since Player's, I peeped off the top that he wanted Alisha on the hush hush. So we made an 'Under

The Table' handshake and his trick ass deposited the ten thousand dollars before he even rung the doorbell.

Threat To The World made an additional thirty thousand dollars to the highest bidder for the virgin. A large white dude wearing a large cowboy hat was eager to pay the large bid as if he just got a hold of a large portion of cattle. Alisha pulled my coat to Chasity's unnerving mannerisms after the meet and greet. She said that she's a student at Lamar college and that she needed to desperately make tuition money for next semester. Chasity contacted Alisha because she initially wanted to work the pole to support her college fund. But after Alisha found out that she was a virgin and that she was willing to compromise her virginity, Alisha had a better idea. I didn't even have to order my bitch to 'Sick Her' because she was already making the bite. And by me being the good Samaritan I am, I felt fortunate that I was able to lend a helping hand. Because after all...A mind is a terrible thing to waste!

CHAPTER 18
COP N LOCK

Sunday morning I woke up three hundred thousand dollars richer, and that was after paying the seven girls I added to the payroll. The 'Three Girl Show' girls were looking pretty nice in the tipping department, so was Alisha. Only they weren't my breadwinners. Who would have ever thought that Maria would be the dark horse that brought in the most tips? I sure in the hell didn't think she would so much as come close to the 'Three Girl Show' girls, let alone Alisha. But the brutal truth is that she smoked everyone by a landslide. For all I know, I failed to spot her potentials because I was giving her the cold shoulder. I wrote her off as nothing but a childish, busybody bitch who needed more than a handful of guidance and I didn't have the time nor the patience to mold her into what I considered to be a first class hoe. Flag on the play, because in the view of the comments from the blogs on our webpage, not only does Maria have boss head but likewise, she's down with the taboo shit that everyone frowns down on. Now I'm beginning to see why Maria and Alisha are so close. Birds of a feather flock together! Now I see the brighter picture. That the secret to becoming an effective pimp is to know the game inside out. First hand, I know to have a hoe in your stable who's willing to do something strange for some change is a pimp's blessing sent first class from the Game God.

Later that afternoon the girls cleaned the house up without Urma's help, due to the fact that she was off on Sundays. Which was cool with me because after they put their heads together, mixed with a little elbow grease, the house was back in mint condition. Maria fell back to lend a helping hand while Shanna gave the Orange girls a lift. At three o'clock we linked up in the computer room.

"Here's the game plan," I said. "Maria, if you want a spot on this team then the first thing you need to get familiar with is how to follow directions. What I want you to do is go to your apartment and pack whatever you can fit into your car, post up and wait on my call."

Alisha, Carmen and Tabatha were sitting calm at each one of the desk while Maria stood before me. She looked back at Alisha over her shoulder as if she was searching for some type of recommendation. All Alisha did was raise her eyebrows but when Maria turned around, she didn't look like her normal merry andrew self. Right now she actually reminded me of Chasity because she was staring down at her hand while she was picking at her fingernails.

"You better call me." She said with her eyes still locked in on her hand. So in a quick, smooth motion I grabbed her by the chin, forcing her to look up at me. In a controlled tone I said.

"I better do nothing except stay a pimp and die, feel me?"

"I feel you papi, it's just that all the other Orange girls got paid except me. How I know you ain't gonna try and burn a bitch?"

I released her jaw then walked over to the desk where one of the tablets was resting. I scrolled down until I found Maria's gross in tips after deductions. I cocked my head, signaling for her to come peep the numbers. When she seen her balance with her own two bulging eyes, I said.

"Everything in life is a gamble Maria, especially if something is at stake with value, but it's just like the game show Let's Make A Deal; I can write you a check for the amount you see before your eyes and you can be about your merry ass way. Or you can hop on this money train and continue playing the game. You got a choice Maria, choose or lose?"

Save the bar, because when I noticed her staring off at nothing with a delayed response, I knew she was hoping for an interruption to avoid answering; so I helped her out a little bit, "Alisha is gonna roll out with you so she can help you pack. Like I said, pack only what you can fit in your car and leave everything else behind. That goes for your fears, doubts and skepticisms too. Leave that shit behind and accept that I don't have time to explain shit in detail. Either you with it or you against it, all I can do is put it in plain English for you…This shit is real Maria!"

"I got her daddy." Alisha said.

"You hit it right on the nose because that's what her

problem is. She wasn't expecting this shit to jump off like this. That bitch ain't never seen that kinda money."

"Ditto!" Carmen said. "It's so funny because just the other day I couldn't imagine any of this, but now I'm really convinced that Threat is like the Pimp Einstein of the new millennium."

Everyone laughed even Maria. Right then I could see her bigger than life personality coming back to fruition. As crazy as it sound, but I wasn't doing any complaining because seeing her down in the dumps was something like watching Jim Carey trying to play a serious role. All you wanted was for the dude to get back into his element. But I can dig it because I guess even Jim Carey would stop telling jokes if someone told him he wasn't getting paid. But there was no way in hell I was gonna give Maria seventy stacks, so basically I had no other option but to Cop N Lock.

I like to consider myself a master pimp psychologist who preys on gullible, weak minded, uneducated bitches so Maria is a prime candidate for a pimp like myself because she could only see my looks, not my strategy. I made an exotic entry in her life, which pretty much sums up why I'm so successful at what I do, because I'm a product of my own craft. In the game of pimping you have to master the art of selling yourself; not like a prostitute contrary to popular belief, but like a politician. In other words a bitch has to be convinced that what you say holds more weight than the actual words of the president of the United States.

Alisha and Maria bounced while I told Carmen to set something up for next weekend. I figured I could kill two birds with one stone because according to our webpage, these tricks are at the edge of their seats and my plan was to keep them captivated by all means necessary. So scheduled for the table next would be what they all seem to want, Maria Valazquez.

A few hours later, Tabatha rolled with me while I negotiated with a few of the most influential muthafuckers I could find in the city of Orange, who so happen to be members to Threat To The World Entertainment. When our huddle was over, I walked away with the address to the location and the green light to put it down. So as of right now it's on; next weekend we'll be right back to work.

By the time I was back at the house, Carmen was running towards the lac waving her hand with gestures for me to open the door. As soon as I opened the driver's side, she said.

"You just missed your sister Maya. She was with some guy in a military uniform. Oh my God they look so cute together."

"What she say?" I asked Carmen as Tabatha was closing her side of the door and I was reaching for my phone inside the console.

"She said she tried to get ahold of you before they left out of town. I think they're headed for some kind of army base or something because she said something about Fort Hood in Central Texas. But she said she would for sure fill you in with details when they get back. You shoulda seen them Threat, they look so happy together. Aww."

When I stepped in the kitchen I noticed I had two missed calls from Maya and one voice mail. I set my phone on the island counter top and listened to her voice message on speaker phone while I poured myself a tall glass of orange juice.

"Edwin and I swung by your playboy mansion." Maya laughed at her sly comment. "I tried to give you a heads up but since someone can't seem to answer their phone, I just came that way to check on you. I'm so glad I came because Edwin is completely blown away by your art. He was all like...Hold on a sec, I'll let him tell you."

There was a slight pause on the line. It wasn't silent because I could hear music flowing from the car stereo. I heard the nigga clear his throat before he got on the phone. Then in a deep tone, almost sounding like Berry White, he said.

"What's up brother-n-law? Well it's not official but it's in the making. But yeah bro, you got skills. I personally like the one you done of Gandhi. What you know about Gandhi? I wanted to ask you if I could pay you to hook something up for ya bro? I'm on leave and Maya is taking vacation time but if you want to talk more about it, you can swing by Maya's house. We'll be back in a couple days. Maya says she has more of your...." Beep.

The voice message discontinued right in the middle of his mumbo jumbo bullshit. I hate when cats try to lay down some type of bond or kinship that wasn't rubber stamped. Nigga I don't know you and you don't know shit about me except what Maya's told you. For this reason alone I would like to ask the nigga one simple question: Why the fuck you calling me, bro?

On the other hand, I had to remind myself that as long

as she likes it then I love it. I can't control her life, true that. And I support her one thousand percent, but that doesn't mean that I have to be part of it. My main priority right now is to stay focused because I knew my next move would be crucial. On top of that, I knew my next move would be my best move.

CHAPTER 19
TRIPLE THREAT

I called Alisha and Maria back on Monday night. Maria looked as if she turned the comedy central channel back on because she was roasting Tabatha non-stop. Alisha on the other hand looked as if she was trapped inside a rerun of Days of Our Lives because she was in a blue funk. Watching her mope around made me feel like I was being tortured by being forced to watch several hours of the Life Time channel. She said that her brother was wilding, committing felonies and terrorizing the whole Orange community.

Word on the street, he's been doing everything from breaking in people's homes, stealing people's shit and rumors of arson. Alisha said everybody and they momma's been calling Mrs. Brusourd with a dispatch on her son's dysfunctional behavior: even the property owner of the house. Now thanks to her son, the Brusourd's have less than thirty days to find somewhere else to live. Damn!

If it ain't one thing, it's another. But, what do you

expect within the lifestyle of a pimp? Drama comes with the territory. Besides, if you want a happy ending then you should get the Disney channel.

All in all, I stayed solid in the face of pandemonium. One thing I know fo-sho is that while it was staring me in the face, I had to double if not triple my money. I told Carmen to schedule not one, but three girls for the table next weekend. Maria, Carmen and Tabatha will be the headliners for our next line up of entertainment. I told Carmen to title the event 'Triple Threat' and as a result, she couldn't hold back her devious smile building up on her face. She leaned in closer to my space, and then with a low whisper she said.

"Priceless!"

Before sundown we held a private ceremony in the bedroom for Maria, we popped a bottle of Dom, poured five quarter full glasses, then I said 'The Pimp's Article of Faith'- All the girls were attentive in their T-shirts and tiny G-string panties while I eighty-sixed my clothes and laid on the bed buck naked. Maria threw her long hair back into a ponytail, grabbed a choke hold on my dick, then she put it in her mouth as I guided her head up and down with my hand while she went to work. 'OOO-WEE man, best believe that Maria is a certified head hunter.

For the rest of the week the voices inside my dome were mild but yet coming in clear like AT&T. "Threat.. Threat…Threat."

I had to ask myself if I were being haunted by a vengeful spirit; someone I fucked over in a past lifetime because in this lifetime I never done anything shysty to not one single living creature. I know Karma is not to be played with. That's why it's obligatory for bitches to know exactly what they're getting themselves into before they get involved with me. I recognize my carnal weakness, my love for the game so I embrace who I am.

Most definitely, a bitch would have to do the same shit. See me as their pimp or take twenty-seven steps backwards with an about face.

For all I know, the voices could be one of the watered down ass niggas in my former crew who dropped a dime on me. Feasibly someone could have smoked one of them quacks so now he's coming at me for holding down my own. I despise a snitch in the same scope that Hitler hated the Jews. Only thing is, I'm allergic to the motherfucker because to me a snitch is two levels lower than a bitch. For this reason, alone I knew I could attract a bunch of negative energy from the hate I practiced. Natural laws are real too and I know for fact that no one can stop the forces of nature.

However, at the same time my hate is equally balanced with appreciation because if it weren't for prison then I wouldn't be the bossed up, game tight, educated nigga I am today. Prison was the best things that ever happen to me. A lot of people fail to realize that every so often negatives can create new positives. Sometimes when you think you're losing, you're actually winning vice versa. Take for instance the turtle and rabbit race. Nough said!

So if it is the bitch niggas who snitched on me that's calling my name, keep screaming it because it's becoming a nice harmonic pitch right at the tip of your tongue like a cheerleader with pom-poms hooraying my success. A clean sweep, I beat the system inside and out. So watch me come out on top and undisputedly have the last laugh while you don't have shit else better to do but yell a pimp's name. "Threat... Threat... Threat"

Saturday Maria was screaming my name too, only she changed it to papi. I wanted to break her in properly while I fucked Carmen and Tabatha the same way. I mastered the art of womanology so it's clear-cut how their physical, mental and moral constitutions operate. See, if you pipe them down good, effective and the right way, then what you did was set the standard for what they consider dynamic sex. Therefore, when a trick runs up in them, then they can't help but fake moans and groans while they're thinking how much better you are at hitting the right spot. A psychological confidence game at its finest, and if you handle up the right way, then how could you be anything less than superman is their eyes?

At ten o'clock PM, we met up with one hundred and thirty-two "Threat To The World" members at the Port of Orange. A ten-acre gravel parking lot was now occupied with stretched limos, SUV's and luxury whips, all parked in a perfect circle with their headlights beaming on three large tables. Maria, Carmen and Tabatha were buck-naked on top of the tables while they were stretched out and staring up at the stars. No stress because our almighty connections made sure this neck of the woods was off limits. Straight-up because not even OPD were allowed on the property. Sometimes it's not what you know but who you know; or better yet, who knows you!

The 'Three Girl Show' girls took flight to Vegas and the Orange girls were enjoying the fruits of their labor. This was all-live because I didn't need them or Khan for this event. I did call Shanna though. She was looking chocolatey smooth with her voluptuous ass and tight physiques while wearing nothing but a white thong and a white neck choker bow tie. Her ass cheeks swallowed the white thong but still she looked like success just waiting on an invitation. She set up all the liquors, champagnes and wines on the hood of her car while she politely made her rounds with a silver platter in one hand and a tablet in the other.

Alisha rocked zilch except a killer pair of spike heels and diamond hoop earrings with glitter sparkling all over her entire body. She never ceases to amaze me because my trophy bottom bitch knew exactly what to do. As she escorted each guest to the tables she walked with an enticing, side-to-side, I'm a bad bitch rhythm.

While they were at the tables set in motion, she prepped the guest by stroking their dicks and sliding the condoms on before, they hopped their horny, libido asses on the table. More than often, she squatted down to a lower position where she was able to give a few of them some of that exotic dome service while they waited in line.

Triple Threat was a beast idea because we made mad, ridiculous money in just a few hours. Not only did the girls receive large tips, but we also drew in donations on a grandiose scale. For the reason that this was our last show in the area, we were able to promote enough chips to where we were now a part of that upper ten percentile. Our guests were generous because in truth they wanted us to see eye to eye with them. As a matter fact, they were thirsty to see "Threat To The World Entertainment" evolve to that next level of what I like to call 'The world Class Fucking Crew'. They were convinced that our team wasn't any every day run-of-the mill bullshit that they were burnt out with seeing every week at Player's. They found an exit. One that opens to a life of exotic fun and pleasure to where they can finally let their hair down and be who the fuck they were without being judged. Pun very much intended!

CHAPTER 20
THE BLUEPRINT

The plan had worked to perfection. Asking a rich motherfucker for money while his dick is rocked up was like taking candy from a baby. Let me get that! But in their eyes, I know they saw us as an investment. They consider us like stock because if a business is seen to be doing well, then the market value can skyrocket above its original par value. This is one way an investor can make capital gains by owning stock. A stockholder also expects to receive an annual dividend based on the profits of the business. Only in our case, they weren't expecting a cash return, more like a sow their royal oats return.

Hey, but I'm cool with that because as of today, I'm two hundred thousand dollars shy of copping my first mill ticket. Not bad for only two months on the street, right? You betta believe it! I knew not to let myself get caught up in a web of contentment because staying hungry right after I just finished eating is the best way to stay full. Ain't no way in hell was I ever gonna sleep on an empty stomach, so not only did I stay hungry I also stayed hoggish.

So that's on the docket this Monday morning, as my Texas homies would say...To hog the lane! After I had a few alterations done to the lac's dashboard, I found a Bentley dealership online. It was in Galveston so I took Alisha with me because I knew I was coming back with something. Does a 2015 Bentley Mulsanne sound a little too farfetched for ya? Well get used to it because that's exactly what I came back with. A metallic gray paint job with white and blue leather guts, the Mulsanne redefined my focus. Taking in a deep breath, the aroma from the leather filled my nostrils and made me feel like I was driving a luxurious spaceship. It's enough room inside the Mulsanne to allow any team to stretch out and it would no doubt be the choice ride for even a basketball goliath such as...Let's see, say 7-foot 2-inch Shaq Diesel. A big body Bentley, a big body bank account with big body ambitions, I'm absolutely where I'm supposed to be. Comfortably reclined, allowing my head to sink in between the wings in the headrest with my bottom bitch tailgating behind.

When we rolled up to the circle driveway I switched positions and sat in the passenger's seat. I turned around and motioned for Alisha to sit in the back. When she opened the back door, she scratched at her temple so I knew she didn't know what was jumping off. Which was better because I was about to lay claims on Maya's Surprise King Title.

"What's going on?" Alisha asked me from the back seat.

"Sit tight." I said as I leaned over and honked the horn with a player ass rhythm that I just came up with off the dome. I had a smirk on my face when all the girls came out at the same time. They were casually dressed in shorts and solid white muscle shirts except Tabatha had a lion on her shirt with glittering black ears and for all I know, a correctly colored nose. She put her hand over her mouth when she said.

"Damn this hoe tight".

"Okay!" Maria said. "Looks like something straight outta a Rick Ross video."

Carmen was shaking her head and right then and there I felt like she wasn't accepting what she was seeing with her own blue eyes. I toyed around with the idea for a few seconds and then dropped it for a momentary vision of what was about to go down.

"No, it fits Threat perfect." Carmen said with her arms crossed over her large titties. She threw a curve at me with that shit, so it was only necessary that I throw one back.

"Everybody get in, but Carmen I want you up front."

Maria and Tabatha hopped in the back with Alisha but when Carmen sat in the front, her mouth fell open when she saw a steering wheel staring at her. I put my hands behind my head and as I clinched my fingers together, I said.

"Now drive".

"No, no, no, c'mon Threat, please don't do this, you know I can't drive."

"It's all in your head Carmen. You can do anything you want to do. Now drive." I said, nodding my head forward.

"But the steering wheel is on the wrong side Threat, it's gonna feel super weird."

"Like I said, it's all in your head. Come on now, we got

shit to do." I leaned over and as I touched the steering wheel, I said. "But if you wreck this three hundred thousand dollar car then there's gonna be a big problem."

"Really? How is something like that supposed to ease my nerves?"

"You're mean papi, that's just wrong." Maria said as she rolled her eyes at me from the back seat. She put her hand on Carmen's shoulder, with a gentle tone she said. "Girl you're not alone, we're all here with you so you can do this".

"This sucks," Carmen said. She gripped the steering wheel so tight that her knuckles turnt pale white. Maria smirked with a soft pat on Carmen's shoulder as she spoke in a quiet voice.

"I suck better!"

When Carmen giggled, I knew Maria's comical shit helped her relax a little bit. She reached back over her shoulder where she was able to grip Maria's hand. Alisha placed her hand on top of theirs with a soothing tone, she said.

"I'm with you too Carmen."

"I am too!" Tabatha said as she reached over Alisha to place her hand on top of everyone's encouraging hands. Carmen glanced in the rearview mirror at everyone in the back seat.

"Thanks guys, I think I can do this."

"You 'Know' you can do this!" I said as I patted Carmen on the leg. "Now come on, let's go."

Carmen looked like she was about to have an anxiety attack as she fastened her seatbelt with jittery hands. Still staring straight ahead, she shook her hands before gripping the steering wheel. She swept her hand across her forehead to get rid of the perspiration then gripped the steering wheel again. She closed her eyes as if she silently said a quick prayer. When she opened them, she said.

"I Can Not Believe I'm Doing This!"

Carmen started the Bentley with mumbles under her breath. She fiddled with the buttons on the side of her door until she found the right one to readjust her seat. She put her left hand on the gearshift and it was obvious to us that this was an awkward position for her to be sitting in the driver's seat on the right side of a spaceship. When she finally put the Bentley in drive, she looked as if she was regaining her confidence because when she eased her foot from the brake, her facial expression said she meant business. She had an alert gaze and she read the road like most people read newspapers. She drove around 10mph down the half-mile stretch until she gained momentum. She reminded me of the little engine that could. "I think I can, I think I can, I think I can."

I nodded my head for her to turn right on the main street, so she hit the turning signal like a pro. One thing I know, that driving a car is like riding a bicycle; it's something you'll never forget how to do. No doubt, because she was handling the spaceship in the league with Captain Kirk. Switching lanes while using the rearview and side view mirrors, watching out for pedestrians and maybe she clean forgot she had a phobia of driving because her observation was on point too. Well, apparently not because when I motioned for her to enter the ramp to I-10, her mouth fell wide open and her eyes were bulged as if she just seen the bitch from The Exorcist in the windshield.

"Oh my God. Oh my God. Oh my God." Is all she kept saying as she stepped on the gas and accelerated on the ramp to the four lane interstate. After about fifteen minutes of driving in the slow lane, she eventually changed course and found herself in the fast lane on an open stretch clearance. When I peeped that she was breathing easy, cool, calm and collected, I hit the radio and right on the money, the proper song for Carmen came to play as Tom Petty screamed at the top of his lungs through the speakers.

"Now I'm free, free falling. Yeah I'm free, free falling."

From then on, it was smooth sailing. I made eye contact with Carmen and when I winked my eye at her, she smiled then pressed on to Beaumont like child's play. She's a natural because being behind the wheel was something ordinary for Carmen. All she needed was that extra push, that incentive to wrap her fears up in a doggy bag and throw that shit out the window. I watched her tilt her head back and burst out in laughter. There wasn't a damn thing funny but it was hilarious to her to see that this was all it took. Think of success like opening that door Carmen! Everything was becoming clear to her, and I hardly doubt that Dr. Phil would even be able to illustrate a picture like this so she could see the light.

When she pulled up behind the lac in the circle driveway, everyone gave Carmen a round of applause.

"Yay, you did it." Maria said. "I knew you could. Now, can we please get out of this car cause I gotta pee?"

Everyone jetted for the house as if they all had the same thing on their mind; Maria was just the only one to speak up. Alisha used the bathroom downstairs so when she came towards the living room, I said.

"Gather everyone up, we're about to huddle up for a minute."

I could hear Urma in the kitchen rattling pots and pans around as if she was about to hook something up. The other day she put us down with a Meyer's lemon chicken sandwich with pulled chicken and roasted pepper aioli. I was taking mental notes about how hard Urma works and how dedicated she is at getting the job done. For a split second, I was trying to decide what I was going to do with her but Alisha was still standing there, staring up at me. I could feel her eyes burning into me. There was silence between us and I could tell there was something on her mental no doubt.

"What's up baby?" I asked her.

"I don't know, I'm just tripping about my momma. I don't wanna see her living on the street due to my retarded ass brother. That boy is so damn triflin, oooh it don't even make sense."

"Alisha let me explain something to you." I said. "First of all, you gonna have to place a little more faith in me than that. We're a family so we catch each other's back right?"

"True, but I don't want you stressing over my issues."

"Your issues are my issues. Your problems, dilemmas and all that shit. If I can't iron them out then I'd be less of a man, feel me?

"I feel that."

"Ah'ight then! Now go get everyone so we can huddle up."

Alisha turned away to collect her thoughts. She opened her mouth to say something but nothing came out. Right then I noticed that she dismissed it with a single wave of her hand. When she ran up upstairs to get everyone, I quickly laid everything out on display. Everything that was in my pocket was now on the coffee table. A couple of minutes later all the girls came down the staircase with their hands on their hips and frowns on their faces as if I just interrupted something important. Well maybe Carmen because she was wrapped up in a towel so it was plain as day that she was about to hop in the shower.

"Okay ladies, this won't take but a minute then you can get back to your extravagant lifestyles. Besides, you can catch Days of Our Lives on the DVR so you won't miss shit. But check game. First, I want to give you all major props for your cooperative efforts by showing willingness to move our team forward. However, remember anything less than the top is unacceptable so understand that where we are now is only but a small fragment of our resting place. In other words, you can make yourself at home but don't kick your feet up because we still have a lot of shit to do, feel me?"

They all nodded their heads in respect to what I just said so now we're seeing eye to eye. In my school of thought, one thing I learnt is that dealing with hoes is like fucking with a seesaw. One minute their up and right before your eyes can blink, they're back down. But the advantage of playing seesaw is to have more weight. Which

I like to think of as authority, inasmuch being in control of their ups and their downs. Mood swings hold no weight over a boss nigga because if you're that powerhouse, all you would have to do is put your foot down on that motherfucking seesaw and then before you know it, they're back up again.

Still, all and all I knew not to come off as a gorilla because a gentlemen's pimp is what I represent. And you know just as well, as I know that with any gentlemen there are rules of conduct. Such as social stability, dignity, protocol, with an influential gift of gab just to name a few. And seeing that my hoes have upgraded to courtesans, it's only proper that I show courtesy by rewarding them with courtesy cards.

"First thing's first." I said. "If you haven't already noticed there are four American Express platinum cards. I want each of you to catch hold of one." As soon as they picked the cards up, I said. "Each card has a thirty thousand dollar spending limit for whatever you like."

"Thirty thousand dollars?" Tabatha shouted out with a rise in her vocal pitch. Maria held the card in front of her face and popped it with her middle finger.

"It's on and popping now, wait until the mall get a load of me, See papi, I have this little weakness for Gucci, so let's just say I'm gonna overindulge."

"Bitch puh-lease." Alisha said. "That knock-off shit you be wearing don't count as Gucci, it only resembles Gucci."

Everyone cracked up but Maria didn't find her being the laughing stock as fun and games.

"Oh, so now you got jokes right? Don't even go there Miss thang, while you tryna front, like you and your momma wasn't poppin tags at Wal-Mart before you got that stripping job."

"Yeah, well that was a long time ago. I'm a big girl now."

"Don't matter; once a Wal-Mart hoe, always a Wal-Mart hoe. You can front like you all miss goody two-shoes all you want, just so you know where home is at."

There was silence between them for a few seconds until Alisha said, "Maria shut the fuck up, okay?"

Maria threw her hands up. "Hey, you took it there bitch, let me find out you can't take a dose of your own medicine."

I didn't speak at first because my eyes we're scanning the girl's energy. To the average eye they could easily come off as if they were locking horns, but it was flat out the other side of the coin. They were in fact excited and bonding with each other right now. Kinda reminds me of how two dogs greet each other. When we see them getting a good whiff of each other's asses, we think all man that's straight up foul. In actuality it's a high-five and salute that, we humans would never be able to comprehend. But I can dig it, I just hope they don't start throwing punches at each other when I pressed on. Carmen and Tabatha were talking in a low pitched volume and bonding on a different level, so I said, "Carmen, pick up the car keys on the table."

She was slow picking up the keys but she automatically knew they were the keys to the lac. After tapping her index finger against her lip several times, she said.

"So you want me to drive the CTS now? At least the steering wheel is on the right side. Well the left side anyway." She giggled. "Cool, where to now?"

"First of all downtown." I said. "Cause what you're gonna have to do is get the lac transferred over to your name."

"What are you talking about?"

"The Cadillac is yours Carmen. There's a picture of your son Kobey on the dash so now your lil man will be with you wherever you go."

Carmen was at loss for words. She glanced down at the keys in her palm as if they held the answers. When she slowly turned her head, Tabatha gave her a thumbs up. She shot her eyes at Alisha.

"Your son kept me company on the way to Galveston. I was wondering why his picture was on the dashboard, but it all makes sense now because he was the best guardian angel."

Carmen didn't come back with a response. She just glanced at me with her crystal blue eyes tearing up as she balled the keys up in her palm and placed her hand to her chest.

"I am so not going to cry right now. But Threat I just want to let you know that you are like the most awesomest guy on this fucking planet. Seriously!" A tear escaped from her eye but she seemed not to care. All she did was made it known that she was flying high because that vibrant smile was lit up like fireworks. I returned the smile then threw my hands up like J.J Evens on Good times.

"Well you know, what can I say?"

They cracked up laughing and I couldn't help but notice that they were looking like little kids in a candy store right now. Once in every blue moon they will catch me bullshitting around and when I did, it was fascinating to them. The way I see it, every hoe needs physical, mental and spiritual therapy so what other treatment is better than laughter? This memorable moment wasn't all about the everyday merry go round ride because I was about to switch gears real quick like.

"Alisha, the last key is for you," I said, but Alisha looked more than confused because her head flinched back and she repeated what I clearly said.

"The last key is for me?"

"Yeah, what part of the last key is for you don't you understand so I can break it down for you?"

"Well, maybe the first, middle and last part because I already have a key to the house."

"But do your moms have one?" I asked her with raised eyebrows so she could catch on that I was giving her an inkling hint to read in-between the lines.

"You mean......?"

"Yeah, that's exactly what I mean! Tell Mrs. Brusourd no stress because she now has a house. I just hope she's on top of her Spanish game."

"Why you say that?"

"Because the maid don't speak a lick of English."

"Aw daddy this is too much." Alisha said. "I can't ask you to give up this house. On top of that, where we suppose to live?"

When I shot my eyes at Alisha and I peeped the expressions on the other girl's face's, I thought about my old man, the boss pimp. His hoes looked at him for all the answers because they knew plus trusted the fact that he was proficient at what he did. He was good at creating a vision in his mind of what could be, then he made it happen. His vision is hereditary because I feel that not only as a pimp but any man should blueprint his own destiny instead of waiting on something to fall outta the sky. My hoes are convinced, just like my old man's hoes were convinced that when it comes to "The Blueprint," we were the master planners so they couldn't wait to see what was jumping off next.

"Girls, brace yourselves for the ride." I said. "Because we're on our way to Dallas."

"Dallas?" Everyone shouted. Alisha was on the hunt for more answers, as she challenged.

"As in Dallas, Texas?"

I winked my eye at Alisha while offering a playful grin. "Is there any other kind of Dallas?"

CHAPTER 21
I NEED A NIGGA LIKE I NEED A HOLE IN MY HEAD

It's about time that I mobilize my stable and spread my wings, because I'm tuned in to the fact that if I can stack almost a mill-ticket in the back woods of nowhere, then just imagine what a pimp can do in a live city like Dallas. I ain't talking about bubble gum, sneaker shoe simping; I'm talking about pole to pole, coast to coast, worldwide pimping. Fake pimps put a black eye in the game because it is easy to convince a hoe that one spot is where it's at. It's called the Mark Zone! There's no such thing as living in a perpetual state of ecstasy just because you're in the game. Furthermore, you can't actually put it into words because pimping is a contact sport. But I can give you an ideal narrative. To be a pimp is to be a globetrotter!

The following day, after Alisha gave her moms and step dad the great news, I shot Maya an e-mail. I told her not to pop up at the house anymore because as of a few hours from now, I no longer lived there. She didn't send a reply but Khan got back at me first thing smoking with an ill temper tantrum. He was throwing a fit, acting like a real live bitch, saying that I planned the short notice on purpose so I could force his hand. He said that my e-mail was an ultimatum because no one gives a hired hand a five-hour notice to pack up and leave everything behind. I was willing to emphasize with the lil nigga until he said the unpardonable, the unforgivable, and the inexcusable shit that I don't turn the other cheek nor accept apologies to. He fucked up when he said that I needed him.

All man, this was most definitely a learning experience for a pimp. I learnt the hard way that when dealing with bitches or niggas with bitch like characteristics, never show interest or even the slightest enthusiasm for a noun; because believe me, at any given time a person, place or thing is subject to be thrown in your face, or better yet, Destroyed.

The interest I showed in Khan came back to haunt me. I flirted around with the potentiality that it could more than likely backfire but I fell short to give it a second thought because I figured my dude was playing with a full deck. But I guess when you're double dealing you could do the trick and pull a fast shuffle on a pimp. It's all live because whatever is in the dark shall eventually come to light, but when it's all said and done, the actual truth is that I need a nigga like I need a hole in my head. Fuck him!

Shanna on the other hand was willing to drop what she had going on to see what I was talking about. I didn't have to twist her arm because she was convinced that I was the answer to her financial miseries. Bottom line, she seen me as Santa Claus or the cash cow that she had a sneaking suspicion she could milk.

Hilarious I know, but still, that's where I wanted her because as long as I knew her intentions then I could help her out with her pimpaphobia issues. One thing I love that no one could ever hold over my head is the invitation to a challenge. Determined to win this bitch, I doubled up my efforts. Thing is, it was my move!   .

CHAPTER 22
WOW

At last, when it was time to roll-out, I asked the girls if they had a problem with Shanna tagging along. Off the rip, no one said anything, they only looked discombobulated from the question I asked. Just when I thought no one was about to speak up, Maria said.

"For what? Anyone can serve alcohol, what she need to do is service to some dick."

Tabatha giggled while Carmen's eyes bucked like she just hit a 50 piece crack rock. Alisha on the other hand had tightness in her eyes when she said.

"Maria, you outta line. I don't know what your problem is but bitch you getting way too comfortable with your mouth."

"I'm just saying."

"No, I'm just saying, shut the fuck up!"

"Listen ladies." I interrupted. "As your pimp I don't owe you any explanation what so ever on my game plan, but as your team captain I see right now that it's important that you know if I decide to act on something, then it was well thought out. But overall, Maria is right. The bitch needs to service to some dick." I chuckled. "I like that! Just remember, before it's all said and done, she will submit, she will toe in line and you will welcome her with open arms. Feel me?"

As soon as Shanna pulled up in her blue Galant, it was time to head out. I told Alisha and Maria to leave their cars here in Orange because the CTS and Bentley was all we needed for the time being.

Alisha rode shot gun with me while Tabatha and Maria sat in the backseat of the Bentley. Carmen trailed behind us with the CTS, which was overloaded with all our clothes, while Shanna chased from the rear. We were on the move, and as we hopped on I-10 I didn't have shit to complain about because after all, I was leaving Orange, Texas in my rearview.

I figure Maya would be straight considering at the present moment she's captivated by a so called love bug. My little sister got it bad. But it's all live because if this nigga she's with is any kind of man then he'll protect her. No doubt because now I feel as though I can be at ease to the point where I don't have to stress about her sleeping with bars on the front door, let alone the damn windows. Furthermore, I already see it coming.

In the near future I'm gonna catch wind that Maya plans to move on base with this fool. The hardest thing to do for any father or older brother when concerning his daughter or baby sister is letting go. As raw as it may sound, but I gotta let Maya do Maya cause I got money to make.

I was in an abyss of thoughts by the time we were exiting 105 W and jumping on I-45 N; the interstate that was going to lead us to the D. From then on it was a straightway stretch where I lead Carmen and Shanna with the Bentley on cruise control.

After several pit stops for gas, food and piss breaks, six hours later we were approaching the metroplex's atmosphere. The Dallas skyline was growing larger and larger the closer we advanced. So was the girls eyes. They looked like they had emerald city in their eyesight, but contrary to The Wizard of Oz, 'There's No Place Like Home' was a motherfucking lie. Dallas symbolized a new beginning, a brighter future, a souped up habitat compared to the shot gun neck of the woods they grew accustomed to. But this was just the tip of the iceberg. Wait until they see Minneapolis and the whole United States abroad.

It was bumper-to-bumper traffic when we hit I-35. The city's prominent skyline dominates with high rises and iconic examples like City Hall, The American Airline Center, not to mention The Reunion Tower, better known as The Ball. Without a doubt it's a recognizable landmark in Dallas. The 55 story Reunion Tower sits on top of the Hyatt Regency. By night the dome is lit up, offering a panoramic 360 degree view of the city. By the way, there's also a dope ass restaurant that rotates on a 55 minute schedule.

"Oh my fucking God." Alisha said. "I heard Dallas was going down but I never imagined it to look like this."

"Okay!" Maria said. "I can really get my swerve on here."

I smirked on the inside as I glanced at Tabatha in the rear-view. She stayed silent, staring out her side of the window while bobbing her head to the Beats By Dre headphones she had on her head. She was in a world of her own but still alert to the fact that she just made a major move in her life. I know she thinks I don't know but she has a birthday coming up. Yeah, I remember everything on her I.D., even the I.D. number. I got a surprise in mind for baby girl that will twist her wig back.

In spite of all the traffic, we finally pulled up to The Dallas-Victory is northwest of Victory Park's American Airline Center but still the W remains in a class of its own. The 62 story building stood solid while we all looked up as we exited and tossed our keys over to the valet parkers. I always wanted to live in the sky with views of the city from every window. Here it is baby.

"Wow!" Carmen said interrupting my thoughts. "I can definitely get use to this."

Which reminded me as we entered the lobby and approached the front desk. Shanna sat down in a red tulip shaped chair in the lounging area while she faked like she was reading an Esquire magazine.

"We have reservations for WOW suite under Thomas Threat" I said to the desk clerk who wore too much makeup. A brunette who had an interesting face, though not a noticeable one. I wouldn't pick her out from a group of bitches to stare at, but still she was fuckable.

"Yes Mr Threat." She said, finally removing her eyes from the computer screen. "You have reservations for an extended stay in the WOW suite number 6226. You should know that we have an open door policy for pets, a full-service, fully wired business center and a whatever/whenever service that will give you exactly what you want, when you want, no questions asked. If you or your guest need anything that we can accommodate you with, please do not hesitate to dial zero on the landline. Thank you Mr. Threat for choosing The W.

When you name rooms shit like Wonderful, Mega, Fantastic and wow, you best not be fucking around. Fortunately, they wasn't fucking around. Stepping foot in the WOW suite number 6226 was a whole experience all on its own. The 1,800 square foot penthouse terrace starts with the decor. It's similarly artful but more futuristic with a midcentury, modern feel to it. Designer's ceiling to floor length rust colored taffeta curtains. And when you open them, you catch a bird's eye view of down-town Dallas from every angle of the suite. A 60-inch Samsung smart TV with wireless speakers is mounted on a stainless steel pole. Goose down comforters and six large throw pillows on a king size bed with an upholstered headboard. Lamps that look like hovering UFO's rest on each side of the bed with a butter-soft leather, cream colored Lawrence sofa that sits at the foot. It's laced with an ample computer work desk with a fly ass leather chair. Two private bathrooms stocked with top of the line sink side products and an extra separate guest room. But what set everything off was the gigantic ass Jacuzzi that was positioned right slap in the middle of the suite.

"I'm not trying to impose on what you got going on Threat." Shanna said. "But do you mind if I could have the guest room?"

Maria twisted her mouth at Shanna's bid for the room and threw up an L sign with her hand indicating 'Loser'. Shanna didn't pay her any attention, she just slid her hands over her ass in her tight jeans then looked around as if she was trying to spot a private area, "And plus I really need to talk to you."

Shanna knew she was turning up the drama dials and the last thing I wanted to do was show favoritism, Shanna knew this, she knew that if she could force my hand she would expose some kind of handicap so I wouldn't appear supernatural to my hoes. I know this shit was better than Jerry Springer to her but it's all live pimpin because playing her game was going to work in my favor.

"That's what's up Shanna." I said, "Go in the guest room, relax and collect yourself, I'll be in there in a minute then we can build, a'ight?"

"Sounds like a plan." She said with a fake smile. "But do you know how long it's going to take for them to bring our clothes?"

Right on cue, there was a knock. I turned my head towards the door then said.

"How bout now?"

Soon after all our luggage and bags was reeled in, I pressed the button on the wall to open the curtains. The sun was going down and blue shadows started falling over the Dallas skyline. The girls didn't waste any time hopping their naked asses in the Jacuzzi, and as I listened to them giggling and laughing with high spirits, I stood in front of the window gazing at the city. I'm right back where I started, I thought; but only now from a bigger and greater standing point. Twelve years ago I was taking penitentiary chances on an South Oak Cliff dangerous block.

Broken street lights, vacant lots, boarded up traps, crack hoes and jackers. I seen all kind of shit in this city. Now I'm viewing it from the sky in a presidential suite with first-class hoes having a blast in a jacuzzi.

"Threat!"

When I quickly turned around and noticed that no one was looking my way, I realized that it came with a price because the voices inside my dome didn't show any sign of letting up. But still, I wasn't about to let it stop me from maintaining my position and most definitely not from living it up. I stared at the girls for a good 30 seconds, then thought: Shanna can wait.

I took my clothes off while I laid out towels by the Jacuzzi. I also laid out several condoms on the nightstand, then I laid down on the bed buck naked as I started with my number one; I said.

"Alisha, dry yourself off and come up here with daddy."

No procrastinating, she was eager to let me tap that ass. I went deep inside her and piped her down missionary style while the other girls observed from the sideline. When Alisha dug her nails into my back, pulling me deeper inside of her, I knew she reached her climax so I told her to go back to the Jacuzzi while I called Carmen up to the bed. I knew Carmen's favorite position was on top so I let her ride. She eased up and down my dick while her large titties were bouncing every which-a-way. I gripped the sheets on the bed to prevent from busting, but when she let off a series of soft moans I knew she got hers. I sent her back then called Tabatha to the bed. Like a kinky little freak, she arched her back and thrust her chest forward while I fucked her full blast from the back. I gripped her hair with my hand, turning her head so I could watch that mixture of pain and pleasure all over her face. While she squirted I thought: Who ever said you can't domesticate a wild animal.

Maria was up to bat. She sucked my dick and it felt so good I almost went into shock. Her mouth was warm, smooth and wet. She deep throated all 12-inches and as she was slapping my dick on her tongue, I turned her around in a sixty-nine position. Maria is the second bitch in this world that can confess that I ate their pussy, and as I exploded all in her mouth, I kept sucking it while the girls watched with their mouths open.

CHAPTER 23
REALITY CHECK

As the night wore on, the girls were exhausted so by 10:00 PM, they were knocked out. It was kinda amusing witnessing them cuddled up with each other on the king size bed. Tabatha and Alisha embraced each other as if they were a couple and Maria held Carmen from her backside. But, somewhere amid all the snuggling and affection, I managed to dip to the guest room.

As a rule, I told myself to never compromise with a bitch and for it to be effortless to toss her up and throw her to the side like a used condom if I had to. This was the moment I knew I had to "turn it up." Adding Shanna to the team is a complement and at the same time, she brings flavor to the stable. But dig, don't get fooled by the smooth taste.

See, I judge bitches on a case-by-case basis. Shanna's energy made her magnetic and her maturity made her stand out from the younger girls, so if I had any intentions on copping this hoe, I had to come from a different angle. Not counting the fact that people always wanted what they couldn't have so the appeal to win this here renegade had my mental spinning in overdrive. When it's all said and done, it's pure and simple; I refuse to lose!

I opened the door and went in with no preconceptions other than to win this bitch. As soon as I opened the door, the incense she had burning filled my nostrils with the aroma of cherry spices and perfume. She also had a respective amount of candles lit in various individual spots throughout the room. With Sade playing on the radio in a low volume coming from the bathroom, I immediately peeped her mental state. More than likely she thought she was one of them neo-soul, Erykah Badu, Jill Scott bitches. But the real truth is that she was looking like she was sweeter than virgin pussy right now. Lying there peacefully sleep on the bed, she was wearing a cut-off T-shirt and a peach thong with white poker dots that exposed every inch of her perfectly round ass.

It goes beyond a stupid booty and a pretty chocolate face. She was nothing short of wicked and supreme. I snapped from her spell and chose to cuff her first thing in the morning because waking a bitch up outta her sleep will guarantee you less than 40 percent. Right now I needed her to be 100 percent wide awake so she could be all ears and on her toes like a ballerina. But as soon as I touched the doorknob to close the door behind me, I was brought to a grinding halt because I heard her say.

"I'm not sleep Threat, I'm only meditating." She took a quick glance at me and seen my hand resting on the doorknob, then as she closed her eyes again, she said. "If your intentions are to torture me, I want you to know that it's definitely working."

Right away, I knew what she was insinuating. The screams, the moans, the body slapping and ass tapping was driving her up the wall; maybe not literally but still, I figure I would give her the benefit of a doubt.

"You coulda came and joined you know." I said half joking but she knew I was dead serious.

"Don't flatter yourself." She said. "Every girl you come across ain't that easy."

"Hmmm, could fooled me." I said as I sat down on the bed. "From my experience, I discovered that pussy is just like money. It ain't shit if you already got it, but it's everything if you don't. But dig, I don't think I ever ran across any stumbling blocks pursuing either of the two."

"Please? Get real! Maybe that's what your problem is, you're so full of yourself that you can't see reality."

"Define reality." I asked her as I crossed my legs and put my hands on my knee. She sat up, now looking more attentive like as if I just touched some kind of nerve or something. She stalled as if she was trying to choose her words carefully and nine times out of ten, she was building up a shield in her mind so she wouldn't come off as open. Finally, she exhaled deeply then said.

"Reality is knowing the difference between a little girl and a 32 year old grown ass woman okay? Sorry to burst your bubble but I'm not one of your silly little whores that you got wrapped around your pinky. Let's just keep it on the biz tip and that will be enough reality for the both of us."

"Thought it was strictly business?" I asked her.

"Yeah, but now you're putting all kinds of extras on it. Look, I just want to make enough money so I can start my own catering service, maybe go back to school or something. Just the basics."

"So that's what you wanted to talk about; little girls, grown ass women, whores, catering services and going back to school? Talking about reality; shit sounds like a reality show."

"Well we can call it The Real World." She said. "Because here in the real world people get paid for their labor."

That shit came from left field but I knew what she was shooting at. Still I asked her.

"What's that supposed to mean?"

"The last get-together, orgy or whatever you call it, I still haven't been paid. I mean, I don't know what you take me as but I don't work for free."

I chuckled but switched to square business real quick like. "I'm gonna shoot from the hip with you Shanna." I said. "It's like this. If you're sweating over chump change then you must need some kinda economic relief. And that's exactly what I'm giving you, a relief from your financial miseries. You do the math. I can easily drop five stacks on you for the last show and an additional two for tips. So if I paid you then what will that make us? Two peas in a pod, right? Because then it would only make sense for you to go fifty-fifty with me on this two thousand dollar a night suite, being that you have your own separate private space, private bath, where you can have your own private thoughts while my silly little whores are bunched up in a bed together. If I paid you and you didn't go half with me on the bill then that means you would be living it up and parlaying in here for free, and ain't nothing in life free but a goddamn dream and when you wake up that shit is gone too."

Shanna went silent and she was slowly shaking her head at me with squinted eyes. There was an unspoken tension between us and for some reason she seemed like she was fantasizing about taking my head off right now. But I stayed solid with my judgment call and I knew she realized that the tables were swiftly turning in my favor. This is chess bitch, not checkers and somewhere down the line she's going to own up to the fact that she's fucking with a motherfucking monster.

"What do you want from me Threat?" She finally asked me, but it was useless to ask because she already knew the answer. I guess sometimes people want to hear it from the horse's mouth, but in my case: The Pimp's Mouthpiece.

"I want you Shanna."

"Me?" She asked with raised eyebrows. "I thought we were keeping it on the biz tip?"

"I am keeping it on a business tip. Everything I do is business, nothing personal."

"Well, if you think I'm about to be one of your whores then you got another thing coming. I don't tolerate that kinda stuff."

"You don't tolerate that kinda stuff?" I asked skeptically. "What do you tolerate? I think it's no coincidence that when I met you, you had a sneaking suspicion that I was a pimp, and now that you know the gospel truth that I am exactly what that is, a pimp! And you're still here? What, you thought I was gonna let you make it and not pursue you? You thought I was gonna piggyback your ass throughout life just because you serve my tricks champagne? And you got the audacity to say I'm full of myself? Bitch, you the one who needs to come face-to-face with reality."

"Bitch?"

"There's no falter in my speech." I said. "I talk clear as faucet water so when did I stutter?"

"So now you want to talk to me like I'm one of your whores huh?"

"Is it any different from you coming at me like I'm some type of trick?"

"Look Threat." She said. "This conversation is getting way out of hand. Why don't we just get some rest and talk about this tomorrow-"

I turned my head with a chuckle, and then I looked Shanna square in the eyes.

"I guess you think you calling the shots up in this bitch too? Right now seems like the perfect time and opportunity to get things straight because sooner or later you're gonna have to catch on to what you're dealing with. Better now than later, feel me?"

"Okay, you wanna go there Threat? You really wanna go there?" She asked me with her hand resting on her hip. "Please tell me, what exactly am I dealing with?"

"A fucked up predicament if you're not careful." I said with another chuckle.

"Please, okay! You're supposed to be this high and mighty pimp who's supposed to be so perfect and so smart. Maybe to those naive girls in there, you're like the universal life force of all living things, but to me? I see right through you!"

I cracked up laughing." You see through me? Is that right?" I asked her, still laughing and wiping a tear from my eyes. "I kind of figured you had a few screws loose but now with your psychic thinking you can see through me. Shit, if anything, all you see is greatness."

I said but Shanna giggled. In all reality, she didn't seem shaken up or the very least sweating what I just shot at her. A matter fact, she had an expression of supreme confidence with a gleam in her eye, an inner light that said she set me up for the kill. In a relaxed mellow tone, she said.

"That's kinda funny coming from a person who hears voices. Can we say cuckoo?"

It was a knife in my stomach, a low blow, a cheap shot that was a cold hard slap to my face. How the fuck did this bitch know what goes down within the depths of my dome? I never told a single soul about the voices. No record of a diagnosis, I never mentioned it to the girls, nothing. Hell, not even Maya knows about my name being called. Before I could interrogate her and go into a full-fledge investigation, she said.

"I pay attention Threat! Also it helps a little bit that psychology was my major in college, so I can pretty much recognize the signs of psychological and behavioral dysfunctions. You have all the characteristics of a man with an antisocial personality disorder. Maybe it started with your childhood or early teenage years, which a long time effect can cause hallucination issues. I noticed how you quickly look up at times as if someone called your name, and then when you realize no one called you, you go back to doing what you were doing. I bet you're not even doing anything about huh? That's what I mean when I say that you can't see reality because in your fantasy land, getting rich and having prostitute is more important than your mental health."

Getting rich and having prostitutes is more important than your mental health carried an echo inside my dome. I stared off at nothing and thought to myself: *Who the fuck is this country, boondocks, back of the woods raised bitch? She's been peeping, analyzing and studying me the whole time. I felt infiltrated. How could a bitch from Orange, Texas make her way inside my dome?*

As soon as I made eye contact with her again, she said. "Don't beat yourself up over this Threat because when it's all said and done, every superhero has a kryptonite. I think you should just focus on what's the most important thing to you and..."

Her double talk and my train of thought was suddenly interrupted by a throat clearing sound. Alisha emerged through the room with my laptop resting under her arm. Her head was down but her eyes looked up and there was a portentous expression on her face. She sat down in-between me and Shanna on the bed and as she opened the laptop, she said.

"I been listening to y'all the whole time and it's a trip because when I first listened I was thinking, *touchy subject.*

But as I continued listening I picked up on everything real quick. They say sometimes darkness can show you the light and that makes sense because it took my brother and Shanna to help me see through you as well."

"You too?" I shouted loud as hell, possibly waking up the other girls. "Where is all this coming from? Huh? Where is all this coming from?" I asked again, but she didn't answer me. She just continued talking as if my voice was on mute or something.

"It all makes sense now. As I think back, I can clearly see what Shanna is talking about. You been hearing voices the whole time. I can't believe this shit...Threat, you're crazy!"

"You stupid little bitches want to jump ship and challenge me?" I said at the top of my lungs as I stood up. "I made every last one of you stank hoes. I bet you wasn't calling me crazy when you was sliding my cards at the Parksdale. You wasn't calling me crazy when I put that white bitch in a new lac. You wasn't calling me crazy when I put your momma in a new house while your pea brain ass brother almost had her living on the street, now was you? Every last one of you punk bitches owe me your goddamn soul. Even that engine bitch in there who I resurrected from the dead. Not to mention the wetback, Mickey Mouse, clown bitch, all you hoes owe me."

Carmen, Tabatha and Maria entered the room. It was now a full audience and ya man was on stage. They stared at me with their arms crossed over their breast with a slow sympathetic shake from their dome. I stared right back at them with my lips pulled back, baring my teeth with an adrenaline rushing through my entire body.

"Show him!" Maria said, still looking at me but talking to Alisha. Alisha surfed the search engine on the laptop until she found what she was looking for.

"Show me what?" I shouted. But Alisha stayed calm when she said.

"What you forgot."

"What the fuck you mean what I forgot? Bitch I got a photographic memory, I don't forget shit."

"Well I don't know about 'Shit', but you definitely forgot about your sister. All because you wanted to be a pimp."

As I opened my mouth to say something, Alisha clicked on the play icon on the YOUTUBE video. My head jerked back when I seen Khan talking through a shaky lense in front of my sister's house. It was at night so he was camouflaged wearing all black but he wasn't concerned about disguising his face. My heartbeat started racing, nearly exploding out of my chest when I seen both Maya and Edwin's cars in the driveway. My eyes were rapidly blinking with dizziness and weakness in my legs and knees. I sat down as I asked in a shaky voice.

"What. The. Fuck?"

"What goes up must come down." Khan said to the camera. "It's one of the many fundamental forces of nature. But I don't have to tell you that because you already know that right? But what you need to understand better is enemies. Rule number one. Never make enemies with someone who is smarter than you because he will eventually discover your weaknesses and use it against you."

The camera was switching positions. All I could see at this point was two pair of black sneakers standing in grass. When the second person came in view, off the top I recognized Alisha's brother. He was also wearing all black with a black skull cap on his head. He was hyper with a lot of goddamn energy as he talked to me through the camera.

"You think you gonna pimp my sister and think it's all good? Nigga I don't play that shit. I'm off the chain nigga. Now you gonna make me go on a rampage nigga. It's straight hood on mine, so pay attention and watch history repeat itself...Bitch!"

Alisha's brother picked up a red gas container and ran towards the house. He had a chain in his other hand so I already knew what was about to go down. My only hope was that Maya wasn't home, that within the realm of possibility she could be in a rental with Edwin. Or maybe all these motherfuckers are working together with some kind of twisted 'Punk'D' venture to stop my pimpin. To actually carry the shit out would be suicide considering their identities are on full blast. Besides, how the fuck is YOUTUBE allowing a premeditated murder to go down on their site with already a hundred thousand existing views? The shit wasn't adding up.

Just when I was about to compose myself, breath easy and enjoy this bullshit spectacle, Alisha's brother most definitely locked the chain on the front door and poured gasoline on the front porch and all around the house, including the garage. Water! Was the first thing that popped up in my dome. But when the lil nigga knocked on the door as loud as he could and struck a match, the house was lit up in flames.

"You paying attention?" Alisha's brother hollered to the camera. "This how it go down in the Fruit. You fuck with one of ours, we fucks over one of yours."

"So this shit is real?" I asked out loud. Alisha didn't say shit, She just stared at the screen with a devilish smirk on her face. The other girls had high chins with hollow poker-faced stares. All at once I felt like I was in some kinda goddamn horror flick or something. My whole world flipped upside down in a matter of minutes. I repeated, "No, it's not real. No, it's not real."

But all my speculations came to a crashing halt when I seen Maya and Edwin screaming at the top of their lungs while frantically shaking the bars with intentions to break free.

"Help, somebody help us!" Maya and Edwin shouted. "Please somebody help us!" But within seconds the house was engulfed in flames to the point where the whole roof caved in. There was an enormous blaze that sent flames and smoke soaring to the sky.

Embers and ashes were flying from the smoke and the blaze appeared aggravated as it torched the house with fierce and murderous intent.

I snatched the laptop from Alisha and threw it against the wall, sending pieces of the keyboard and plastic flying everywhere.

"You hoes got me fucked up, I'm gonna kill every last one of you bitches with my hands." I said. But there was an unnatural silence. They looked like they were unfazed by my barks and death threats. They appeared hypnotized like they were under some kind of fucked up spell. Shanna giggled.

"Seems like there's a pimp in distress."

They all laughed while my mind was struggling with belief: This can't be happening! My thoughts searched for a solution but the shit was moving too quick to process. I received chest pains while my hand flew to my chest. My heart was giving out and I was having a panic attack all at the same time. I was holding back a scream but the one inside my dome let it rip.

"Threat...Threat...Threat"

I felt a sudden rush of claustrophobia with sounds of my heartbeat thumping in my ears. Shaking my head in denial while clapping my hands over my ears. The voices were coming strong and clear, now for the first time I heard something else besides my name being called.

"THREAT..WAKE UP!!!!!"

CHAPTER 24
I BELIEVE I CAN FLY

I woke up to my eyes staring up at a hospital ceiling. I felt trapped. Not because I was laying in a hospital bed, but because my wrist was handcuffed to a damn rail. Right at that moment I felt worthless, like someone erased my brainpower and replaced it with some half-baked nigga's brain. I was short-sighted and my thoughts were simple. My body felt fragile and puny. I ain't lying cause I felt like a two-bit small fry who couldn't even match up with Peewee Hurmen right now. To top it off, I felt pigeon hearted because I almost jumped outta my skin when I heard someone say.

"Oh my God, he's woke, he's woke, he's woke!"

When the beautiful face came hovering over me, my eyes lit up like a Christmas tree.

"Maya, is that you?" I asked with disbelief.

"What kinda crazy question is that? Of course it's me, who else would it be? I been here with you the whole time. But whew!" She sighed dramatically and wiped invisible sweat from her forehead. "Please do not ever do that again, you hear me?"

"Do what?" I asked, not having the slightest clue of what was going on.

"You came up with a bright idea to stop taking your medication and well let's just say you had an episode and took a nasty blow to your head. You've been in an coma for sixty-two days and I been calling your name from day one. I knew you would come through, I just knew it."

I raised my hand where the handcuffs jingled against the rail and I asked her, "Why the handcuffs?"

She gave me a playful pinch to my chin, with a giggle she said, "Because you're in prison silly. Don't you remember anything?

The Mumford unit is a hospital but it's actually a prison too. But the guards are cool. They said that if you wake up, and I always corrected them; that 'When' you wake up, they said your visitation privileges will be limited to weekends only. But I'm pretty sure this very nice officer right here will let me stay for a little longer, right?"

She shot a winking hint and directed my attention to a white, over weight TDCJ guard who was sitting down in a chair while peacefully reading a newspaper. He showed the slightest concern about me being woke right now. All he did was lower the newspaper from his face with a nod towards his watch. When he raised the newspaper back up to his face, I asked Maya.

"How long have I been in prison?"

"Six months." Maya said. "You have eleven years and six months to go. But it's too early in your sentence to be worried about time don't you think?" She asked with a giggle.

But at this point I'm thinking: *Six months? You mean to tell me it was all a dream? My education, my talents, my freedom, my physique, all the way to the super-duper pimp I learnt how to be? But I was so good at it. I took the game to outter limits. How could it be a dream when it felt so real?*

My thoughts were interrupted by a Middle Eastern doctor who approached the bed wearing a white coat, a stethoscope around his neck and a clipboard in his hand. He was short with solid black hair and it was slicked back just like...Oh snap! this dude was an exact replica of Muhammad in my dream.

"Good to have you back with us Mr. Threat." The doctor said. "You experienced an intense head injury and any hard blow like that will quite naturally cause a disturbance to your cerebral functions. Unfortunately you do have a concussion because the trauma to your head was so severe, you may also experience symptoms of amnesia. However, the good news is that there's no sign of permanent brain damage, as is the case with posttraumatic amnesia. You may even forget who you are but no need to panic because your memory will slightly develop over time." He patted me on my shoulder with a sympathetic expression, he said. "You're one lucky camper to have a sister like Maya. She never left your side except to eat and change clothes, and she was literally forced to do that. She created a system to where she called your name three times every hour and when she had to leave she made sure there were substitutes."

"She made me call your name." The TDCJ guard said from behind the newspaper.

"Including our entire six floor nursing staff." The doctor said. "When you're fortunate to have support like your sister, there's no way possible you can ever resort to criminal behavior. That's great! Anyway, Mr. Threat, we will monitor you for 72 hours then you will be transferred over to the psych department for further evaluation."

"The psych department?" I asked with raised eyebrows.

"Yes Mr Threat." The doctor said reading from his clipboard. "You were diagnosed with a psychosis mental illness when you were housed at Allred Unit."

"What the hell is that?" I asked, attempting to connect the pieces to the puzzle.

"Psychosis is any mental illness, whether of neurological or purely psychological origins that impairs your ability to distinguish reality from fantasy."

"What?" I asked while I scratched my head with my free hand.

Maya smacked her lips. She looked like she had a dying need to break down what the doctor said in layman's terms. She sighed then said, "Look Threat, you thought you were Superman when you leaped from two row. No telling who you thought you were in your dream."

About The Author

Richard Spraggins is an aspiring author who is best known for his artwork. He is currently working on his second novel and a new style of art which (like himself) is in the process of perfection.

We Help You Self-Publish Your Book

Made in the USA
Columbia, SC
19 February 2023

12283844R00150